# LIVE
## LIKE YOU
## ARE
# DYING

# LIVE
## LIKE YOU
## ARE
## DYING

**Make** Your **Life** Count
**Moment** by **Moment**

HARRIS KERN

RUPA

Published by
Rupa Publications India Pvt. Ltd 2019
7/16, Ansari Road, Daryaganj
New Delhi 110002

*Sales centres:*
Allahabad Bengaluru Chennai
Hyderabad Jaipur Kathmandu
Kolkata Mumbai

ISBN: 978-93-5333-563-2

First impression 2019

10 9 8 7 6 5 4 3 2 1

The moral right of the author has been asserted.

This edition is for sale in the Indian subcontinent only.

# Contents

# Introduction

At a very young age, I was told by my neighbor to "Act as if you're going to die at 40 years old and live life accordingly." This philosophy resonated with me and set me on a path of living with urgency and to chase success in every facet of life. Almost accidentally, I stumbled upon the importance of *discipline* in leading a successful life. This "Pig-Headed Discipline (PHD)" coupled with the dark thought of dying at forty compelled me to create that extraordinary life.

At the tail-end of authoring my latest book on the topic of self-mastery, I had an epiphany: How come so many of us in life 'don't treat time with more respect? Simply because we think we have an infinite supply of it. The harsh reality is that the age "forty" will come and go before we know it, and the chances of true success after this milestone diminishes greatly for the vast majority of people.

My epiphany caused me to re-evaluate my message; being disciplined is great, but people need to better understand why they truly need it. Simply put, we all die. Sure, many of us live well into their eighties and beyond, but you never know. If the vast majority of us adopted the philosophy that our expiration date is at forty years, how much more focused would we be with our early lives? We'd better understand why we need discipline in order to achieve everything we want before we kick the bucket.

Granted, my message may sound morbid to many, but those who feel that way are kidding themselves and shying away from the fact that my message is the kind of *reality* that *really* hits you in the gut. Based on my past experience as a life coach, people don't want to hear *reality*. What they truly want is to hear positive thoughts and to be provided with quick, easy solutions to their weaknesses. I had the dubious pleasure of setting the record straight. There are no quick fixes, and instilling structure into a chaotic lifestyle isn't easy.

Throughout my twenties and thirties, no one knew that I had a war brewing internally. I was always positive and jovial on the outside. Inside, I was in a constant battle to outperform my previous best every day. I needed to accomplish more, and faster. I knew my time was limited and all I could do was think but one word: *legacy*. I wanted to leave my family more than just pictures. Well, I'm in my early sixties now, and there's still a sense of urgency.

This book is a bit of an autobiography celebrating the trials, tribulations and achievements I had during my first forty years of life and how my sense of urgency pushed me forward through adversity and to achieve the things in my life that most people only dream of. I have also been collaborating with a host of celebrities who were guided into their success by the same philosophy...pretend as if you're dying at forty years! How many of us would like to:

- Buy a home before the age of twenty
- Appear on the cover of a magazine because of a hobby or passion of ours

- Climb the corporate ladder without a formal education
- Live a life of healthfulness and prime physique
- Visit exotic people and countries around the world
- Mentor hundreds of people and dozens of organizations to become more efficient
- Start a successful business while working as an executive at a large corporation
- Own an expensive luxury sports car in our thirties
- Manage sleep optimally
- Have financial security in our thirties
- Publish dozens of books with the largest publishing company in the world while working twelve-hour days as an executive
- Purchase (in cash) a brand new car at the age of sixteen

The foundation for all of these achievements must be laid early in life. The mistake most people make, at least from what I have seen, is that they waste time. They're deluded into thinking that success will come—somehow miraculously appearing one day. The truth is very different.

When you're in the prime of your life, which is the late teen years, twenties and early thirties for most (not based on scientific data—however, a majority would agree), there seems to be plenty of time to have a great career, buy a home, start a family and invest for your retirement. Even if you're only thirty, you still have approximately fifty years to make your dreams come true, right? Think again!

Most people these days don't sweat it if they're not able to complete that project today—tomorrow's another day, after all. *What's the rush? Life is too short, sometimes you just have to stop and smell the roses.* It is this kind of mentality prevailing on a universal level that makes *procrastination* by far the number one deterrent to success.

Well, here's a spoiler alert for all you teens, twenty- and thirty-somethings—your biological clock is ticking away as you read this. The first forty years of your existence sets the tone for the rest of your life, so if you haven't accomplished most of your dreams by this age then the chances of you doing so greatly diminish as you exit your prime years when your power and vigor are greatest. Contrary to popular belief, you actually only have until the age of forty to make something special happen in your life.

There are numerous opinions about when the prime of your life actually occurs; for me it was my late teens through my twenties to my mid-thirties. However, that doesn't mean that I stopped accomplishing things in my forties. On the contrary, what changed for me was more physical, not mental. I depended heavily on my exercise routine each morning to set the tone (mental and physical efficiency) for my entire day.

I had a rigorous weightlifting regimen, and in my forties, body ailments were more frequent, and recovery time was much longer than in my prime years. Also, in your forties, your muscle mass decreases and your amount of fat tends to increase, decreasing your BMR and the number of calories your body burns. Also, the issues associated with your personal and professional life seem to intensify with age (large families, which typically means more drama, additional assets to manage, and perhaps multiple businesses).

Of course, that is not to say that there haven't been individuals who have accomplished great things beyond forty. For example:

- Ray Kroc was a milkshake device salesman before buying McDonalds at age fifty-two.

- Henry Ford was forty-five when he created the Model T car.
- Julia Child launched her career as a celebrity chef when she was fifty.
- Harland Sanders, better known as Colonel Sanders, was sixty-two when he franchised Kentucky Fried Chicken in 1952.

That's an awesome list with many others who have been successful post-forty. However, these high profile names are far and few between. Ask yourself: *Are you one of those young or not-so-young people who have adopted a lackadaisical approach toward life and the passing of time?* Do you think you have all the time in the world to become successful? Has it ever occurred to you that your life has an expiration date? The time has come for you to stop fooling yourself. The crux of the matter is, we all have something in common—we will all die—some sooner than later. None of us know when our last day on this earth will be. You have two clear-cut choices here: Exist only for today or go for the gusto and *live the most meaningful life you can build!*

## EXIST FOR TODAY OR LIVE FOR TOMORROW

Most people simply exist. They live life on a day-to-day basis, doing the bare minimum. Despite their lack of zeal for living, they somehow manage to squeak by. They will waste time like there's an abundance of it; by surfing the Internet aimlessly, watching TV for hours at a time and playing video games until their fingers ache. As if this isn't bad enough, they will also squander more of their time on irrelevant conversations throughout their day. Since these individuals are not structured, meaning they do not follow a to-do list, a formal routine, are not punctual and are disorganized, they're always unproductive. To make matters worse, they use the same old lame excuse: *there are never enough hours in a day.* These are *The Existers* of this world.

The Existers don't really plan out their lives—and if by chance they give it a try, it's usually done haphazardly. They don't have a sense of urgency, they rarely accomplish their goals, and they have a difficult time motivating themselves. If that's not enough time flushed down the toilet, it gets worse on the weekend. It starts by lounging around in bed and it goes downhill from there. See Appendix A for some of the Existers' favorite anecdotes.

So, here is a loaded question for you. Do you want to exist like the parasites of the world, or would you rather live life with real passion? If you want to barely scrape by in life, then stop reading any further. However, if you want to *really thrive* and be successful by the age of forty, then by all means continue reading to learn how to *live like you are going to die.* See the Appendix for my favorite anecdotes for individuals who want to live like they are dying.

I only ask that you keep an open mind. My message comes from the heart and wholly unique life experiences. I am passionate about helping people become successful, especially the youth of today.

## DO OR DIE!

Why do many individuals think age forty is a make-or-break number for success? Forty is considered old by society's standards, such as getting into the military, starting a new career, graduating from college, getting married for the first time and starting a family. There is no rule set in stone that says you can't do these things at or past the age of forty. The trouble is society *thinks* you are too old to *start* at forty. I also strongly believe it's much more difficult than starting something in your thirties. Typically by this age you've either made it in life or haven't—and the odds are that if you haven't, then you might not make it at all.

Let's say you are twenty to thirty years old, and you know you are destined to die in ten or twenty years, as opposed to living for another half a century. Wouldn't you do everything within your power to accomplish your goals as quickly as possible? Wouldn't you make it your top priority to leave behind a legacy for your loved ones? Wouldn't you stop procrastinating once and for all and live your life with urgency every day? Of course you would!

Why not train your mind to believe that life does actually end at age forty? If you were able to program your mind into thinking that you will die at forty, then that sense of urgency will become very real to you and you'll jump through hoops to get things done.

Creating a sense of urgency allows you to draw upon greater resources. Think for a moment. It is necessity that gets your mind working. Remember that saying—"Necessity is the mother of invention"?" We all can accomplish miracles when we feel strongly about something.

If things are too comfortable for us, we tend to coast along, forgetting that time is passing, oblivious to the fact that we are not accomplishing our goals. We get distracted. We complain about our food not being cooked right. We obsess over whether we made the right decision.

It is the sense of urgency that allows us to tap into resources we didn't even realize we had. You must have seen an athlete performing a miracle in a sports game, or a rescue worker such as a fireman going back into a burning building to rescue someone.

## DOING MORE WITH LESS

*"Don't be fooled by the calendar. There are only as many days in the year as you make use of. One man gets only a week's value out of a year while another man gets a full year's value out of a week."*

**—Charles Richards**

Each day has become a substantial challenge for the young and the elderly alike. Whether you're nineteen years old (going to school, working a full-time job or participating insocial activities) or in your early fifties (with a full-time job, kids and errands, or as a cook, educator or homemaker) there are never enough hours in a day to finish your daily activities. All that time is spent just maintaining your current lifestyle. Consequently, many of your daily chores and responsibilities get pushed to the next day. What about new goals and objectives? Forget it—who has the time? You're always trying to play catch up instead of getting ahead of the game. You've become a slave to your daily routine.

The pressure is all around us, from the business world to our home life. Our society goes non-stop. At work, management is cutting back everywhere except on the workload. Corporations are getting mean and lean by cutting back on the number of employees. The job functions are still the same, but your employer hasn't cut back on your responsibilities, yet you're expected to pick up the slack. This seems to be the common theme these days. Accomplishing more with less time and resources has become the norm for all of us.

At home, both adults are usually working. The kids want your time—you have to eat—someone has to cook—so nighttime consists of surfing the Internet, checking email, or whatever. In addition, oh yes, I almost forgot, you would really like to exercise on a regular basis. Something has to give. Like it or not, the pressure will only get worse. The only way to get ahead is to continuously motivate yourself every day to drive and push yourself like never before. But that's easier said than done.

Your body will need to be in superb physical condition. Whether you like it or not, you won't have a choice but to cut back on some of the simple pleasures life has to offer (i.e. sleeping nine-ten hours, watching football all day on Sundays or sitting around doing nothing). Work will not let up, and neither will the kids. Will it ever get better? No. It will not. Industry competition and economics will continue to push the employer to get more out of their employees. Doing more with less is now a way of life. Whether it's at home or work, you have no choice.

> "Don't be afraid your life will end; be afraid
> that it will never begin."
>
> **—Grace Hanson**

As I travel the globe meeting thousands of people a year, it's frightening to see how many individuals can't get ahead in life. Most of them want to accomplish more than they currently do. Some of their most common remarks are:

- "I have limited bandwidth."
- "It's hard enough just maintaining my current lifestyle."
- "I'm too tired at the end of the day."
- "There aren't enough hours in a day."

I happen to agree with most of these points above. However, you can keep complaining about your workload, time, energy, obligations and projects, or you can change your lifestyle to accommodate the fact that doing more with less resources is here to stay.

## YOU HAVE THE POWER

Do you really like what you see in the mirror? Are you happy with your current lifestyle? Would you like your life to be a bit more organized? Wouldn't you like to have a few extra hours at the end of each week? Would you like to be motivated every day of the year? Do you wish you could be consistent with your priorities? Do you wish you could be sincere about your commitments? Do you wish these questions would end? I'm sure you answered yes to all of these questions. You have the power to build these characteristics and others that are equally important. Being disciplined to live life with a sense of urgency is not hereditary; it comes with hard work.

You have the power to make what you want out of your life. Make your life challenging, and excitement will naturally follow. Life is so precious. Why waste it? Live it! Come on, I know it sounds like a cliché, but "be all you can be." So, get on it—what are you waiting for? If you refuse to accept anything but the best, you'll always get the best. Begin to live life as you wish to live. You have no idea how much power your mind and body possess; if trained properly, you can take on anything. Never underestimate the power of your mind.

## A SPECIAL MESSAGE FROM THE AUTHOR

*Live Like You Are Dying: Make Your Life Count Moment by Moment* is divided into two major sections:

1. Prescriptive
   a. Training your mind to live like you are dying
      i.   Setting an expiration date
      ii.  Playing mind games
      iii. Treating every day equally
   b. Instilling a sense of urgency in our teens
2. The Author's Case Study
   The proof, not the hype (personal and professional)

For those of you who prefer a different view:

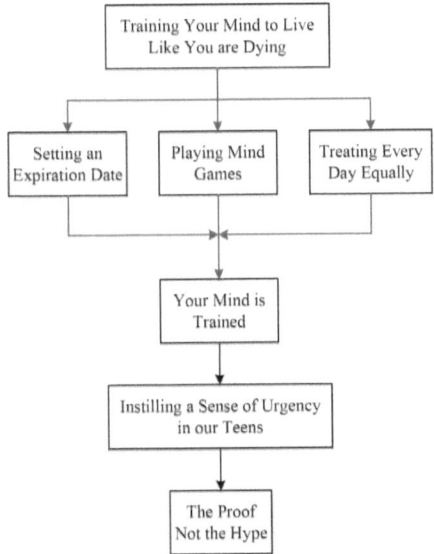

Whichever depiction you prefer, my objective is to keep the message in this book simple.

The *prescriptive* section is where the rubber meets the road. This is precisely why I felt compelled to dish out the beef (How to...) of my overall message first. *Training your mind* to think with a *sense of urgency* every day of the year is the key to success. It's life-altering. It's a necessity in this era of always trying to do as much as possible in a 24-hour period, while trying to accomplish your short and long-term goals. Training your mind to think with urgency is the best method I could find that worked. Without this urgency, you will be like most people I meet along the way, who procrastinate as if time were infinite.

The *Author Case Study* section is my life story. It's the *proof, not the hype* about how to live life with a sense of urgency. This section is divided into two parts: professional and personal. I believe it's important for you to read about my plight.

I cordially invite you, the reader, to write to me. I would absolutely love to hear your opinions, comments, suggestions, complaints or even ideas for the kind of book I should write next. I can be reached at harris@harriskern.com.

# PART I

---

# HOW TO LIVE LIKE YOU ARE DYING

# Training Your Mind to Think with a Sense of Urgency

Why would anyone in their right mind want to be in a hurry every day of the year? Why would you want to rush through life? And if you live life with urgency, does that mean you can't slow down enough to enjoy the fruits of your labor? I've been living life with urgency for the past forty years, and just because this mode of operation allows me to accomplish a great deal doesn't mean I don't enjoy myself.

I take vacations like everyone else. I spend quality time with God, with my family, and exercise every day. I also work on three of the businesses I love. The bottom line is that I live a balanced, fun and rewarding lifestyle. I just accomplish more than most people because I live life with urgency.

## LIFE IS ALL ABOUT ACCOMPLISHMENTS

When will people stop denying or ignoring that we're on this planet one time and *one time only?* We are all given but one life to live, and if we should happen to botch it up, there are no "do-overs". Pull this undeniable truth out of the deep caverns of your mind and bring it to the forefront. It should be a constant reminder that time is our most precious commodity. I continually ask myself, *Why are millions of people wasting so much time every day?* I can't imagine not accomplishing one goal after another (major and minor) until the day I leave this world. If there are no accomplishments, there is no life, or at best it's an unfulfilled life. There is no purpose for living. You may exist, but that's not living. Living is progressing, not merely breathing.

There is no greater feeling in the world than accomplishing a major goal. Once you complete a goal, you will never forget it. It's hard to describe, in mere words, what the feeling is like. It's a kind of euphoria that not only makes you feel invincible, but is extremely addictive as well. The level of intensity is relative to the difficulty of the goal. The harder the goal, the stronger is the feeling of accomplishment. I still remember each and every goal, even the ones I accomplished over forty years ago.

Living life with urgency or as the title of this book states, *Live Like You are Dying,* will allow you to accomplish more. However, to *consistently* live life with a sense of urgency requires taking extraordinary, hardcore measures to train your mind to consistently motivate you.

## LIVE LIKE THERE'S NO TOMORROW

Time is our most valuable resource. You can waste it or invest it. When it's gone, you can't get it back. You have one lifetime to play the game you're currently engaged in. So, the moral of this story is to treat time as the precious resource that it is and utilize it fully.

Be in survival mode every day of the year! Give yourself deadlines, and not only meet them but better yet *beat them*! One of the tricks the mind plays on you is with time. Your mind will say things like, "I have plenty of time to complete my goals—I'm only *xx* years old," or "I still have three months to complete my goal—what's the rush?" The trouble is that tomorrow comes and the goal has not been met. It's a deceiving and damaging cycle that must be broken.

You never know when the unpredicted will impact your life and something happens that changes everything; a death, an accident, a stock market crash, a natural disaster, a major illness. You need to play mind games with yourself because the outside world likes to steal your time and the saboteur inside uses the same mechanism.

Convince yourself there is always the possibility of an emergency and then tell yourself repeatedly to accomplish that goal quickly before that potential emergency blindsides you.

There are several methods to instill a sense of urgency as illustrated in the graph below. I used all three to train my mind to achieve the ultimate level of efficiency and productivity.

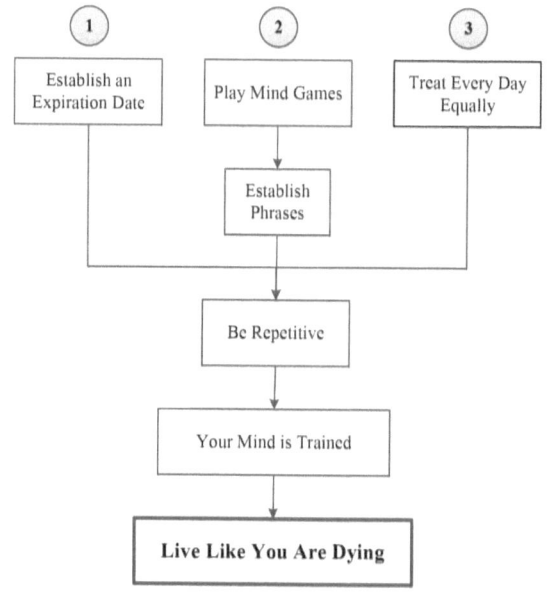

## Set Your Expiration Date

One of the most effective ways is to live every day like you truly have an expiration date, just like any carton of milk. Trust me, it works like a charm. I approached my mentor in my early twenties and asked him how I can *consistently* do more in a shorter amount of time. He said, "Believe you are going to die soon—that you actually know when you are going to die." I looked at him like he had two heads instead of one, but never questioned him and never looked back.

Based on my major goals, I decided to pick the age of 40 as my expiration date. When you're in your early twenties, the age of forty seems old. I kept telling myself to hurry because I was going to die at forty. I kept telling myself this daily—actually several times a day. I wanted to give myself a deadline to complete my major goals as quickly as possible. I also wanted to leave behind a legacy for my future kids. I've seen too many elderly people who had given up on their dreams, too many people with regrets because they didn't complete some of their most important goals. I didn't want to be another statistic. I pushed *hard*. I actually accomplished the following major goals before the age of forty:

- Have at least one million dollars in cash and one million dollars in assets
- Own at least three homes
- Pay cash for a luxury car
- Become a Vice President in a major corporation
- Travel the world
- Publish a book
- Have one of the top muscle cars in the nation. I was a muscle car and speed boat fanatic. I wanted to own the ultimate car and boat with matching paint jobs. They actually graced the cover of the *Hot Rod* magazine in July of 1975.

I'm not saying you have to take it to this extreme, however, this is your life and none of us know how much time we have. So use your time wisely and abhor waste. Below is an illustration of someone who lives life with urgency with the priorities of *health*, *career* and *relationships* and that same person who doesn't live with urgency going down quickly.

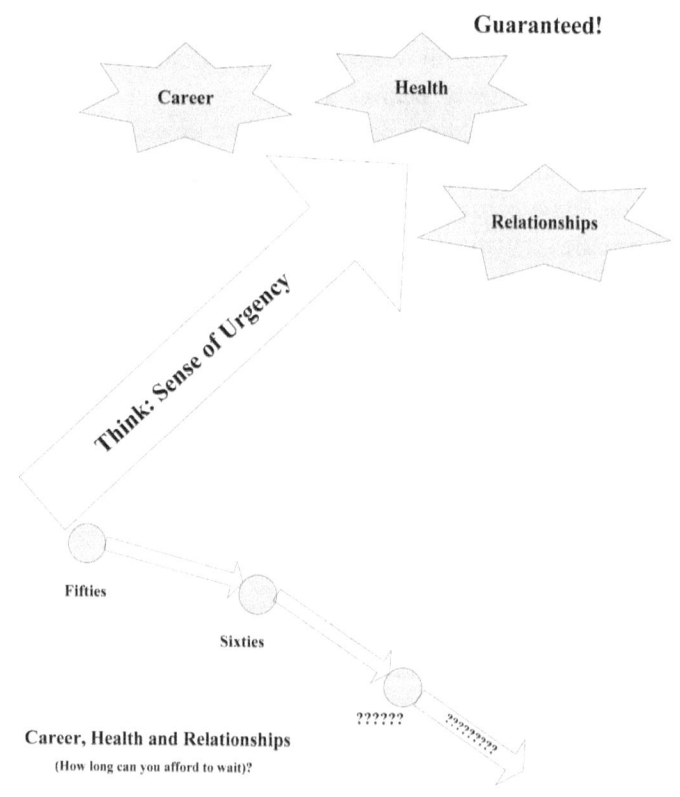

## Believing You Will Die at Forty

Believing you will die at forty is life-altering. You will be in a different mode of operation than anyone else. The benefits depicted below are second to none.

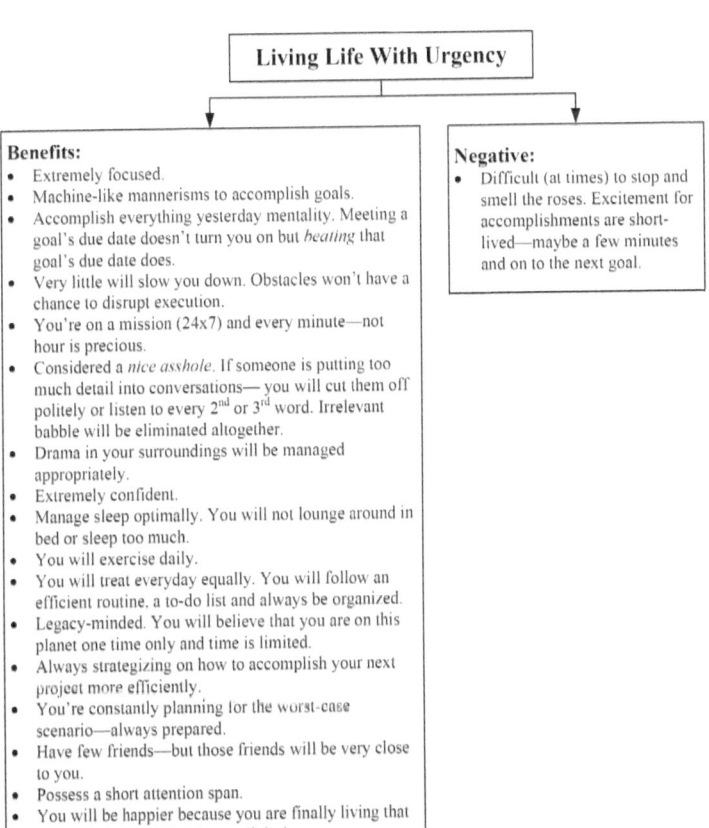

| **Living Life With Urgency** |

**Benefits:**
- Extremely focused.
- Machine-like mannerisms to accomplish goals.
- Accomplish everything yesterday mentality. Meeting a goal's due date doesn't turn you on but *beating* that goal's due date does.
- Very little will slow you down. Obstacles won't have a chance to disrupt execution.
- You're on a mission (24x7) and every minute—not hour is precious.
- Considered a *nice asshole*. If someone is putting too much detail into conversations— you will cut them off politely or listen to every 2$^{nd}$ or 3$^{rd}$ word. Irrelevant babble will be eliminated altogether.
- Drama in your surroundings will be managed appropriately.
- Extremely confident.
- Manage sleep optimally. You will not lounge around in bed or sleep too much.
- You will exercise daily.
- You will treat everyday equally. You will follow an efficient routine, a to-do list and always be organized.
- Legacy-minded. You will believe that you are on this planet one time only and time is limited.
- Always strategizing on how to accomplish your next project more efficiently.
- You're constantly planning for the worst-case scenario—always prepared.
- Have few friends—but those friends will be very close to you.
- Possess a short attention span.
- You will be happier because you are finally living that elusive balanced lifestyle we all desire.

**Negative:**
- Difficult (at times) to stop and smell the roses. Excitement for accomplishments are short-lived—maybe a few minutes and on to the next goal.

Living life knowing and believing that you will die at forty definitely has some incredible side effects.

## Play Mind Games

I've been playing mind games to properly train myself for over four decades. It has proven to be my greatest ally in becoming successful. Mind games are lines you repeat over and over again until they become permanently entrenched in your mind and become part of your life. Silly as it may sound, they are the main ingredients to help you accomplish your goals. This process may sound crazy, and some of the lines you use may sound ridiculous, but the process works! People often ask me what my secret formula is for being so disciplined and accomplishing so much in life. I tell them that I talk to my mind and it barks out orders at me all day long. Yes, it's only one voice, and no. I'm not a schizophrenic or bipolar!

It's so much more than training my mind to guide me when I need it the most. These little lines are automatically and subconsciously played back in my mind at appropriate times repeatedly. The appropriate time is when you need that little extra push to help you accomplish those tasks, obligations and milestones for any given day. My mind doesn't speak to me in a soft gentle voice. It's more like a drill sergeant's voice never letting up, and continuously bombarding me 24/7. The sergeant is relentless—he never tires. My mind is no different. It never eases up or gives me a break. It's unyielding to guarantee my success. Maybe I trained it so well that I have been labeled a machine in my pursuit of accomplishments. But others also know without a doubt that I am a sensitive and caring individual as well. They know I am a man of my word and I will not waiver from accomplishing set goals.

This sounds so farfetched; why should you believe me? I started with practically nothing. I barely passed high school, was pathetically skinny, and lived in a very poor neighborhood. Today I'm an author, publisher, life coach, businessman, IT consultant, speaker and playing my most important role—a family man—with more accomplishments than most people would have in two lifetimes. I attribute it to training my mind to live life with a sense of urgency.

Yes, I still play mind games to train myself further to accomplish more, even at the age of sixty. The mind is your best tool to help you accomplish much more than you ever thought possible. My greatest ally, companion, confidant, etc. is and always will be my mind. Training your mind is best described as a series of premeditated steps that you take to evoke a desired behavior. Whereas you train a muscle to perform a desired movement or motion, you train the mind to obtain the desired concentration and attitude, as well as to defeat laziness.

It's difficult to motivate yourself *every* day of the year. The only way to push yourself consistently is to train yourself to push your body for you. Once you have done so, you will consistently hold yourself accountable and be successful in all your endeavors. Motivation will constantly nudge you forward even when you're tired and feeling lazy.

You will rarely get tired or need a break, so take advantage of it. When trying to do more with less you need every tool you can get your hands on. The sooner you harness its strength to work in your favor the better. Then the sky is the limit.

Is it hard work? Without a doubt it's one of the most difficult things you'll ever do. Nothing this rewarding will be easy. Will it ever let you ease up? Sometimes, but only after your milestones, tasks and obligations have been completed for that day. Don't think of this as a hobby or a side job. It's a full-time commitment—a business plan to be followed precisely and effectively.

Establish Lines (to play mind games)

Choose lines that will have an impact on you and are easy

to remember. I used lines that were *very* negative, to light that much needed fire under my pants. You can't get much more negative than: *I will die at 40*. I went for the gusto to help me get that extra edge (i.e., purpose, motivation, attitude, etc.). Just because I used negative lines didn't mean I was a grouch all day. My personality was the complete opposite. I was always cordial and nice to everyone. On face value no one could tell I was using negativity to motivate myself. This method of training my mind was between me, myself and I. Yup, there was a battle brewing daily to combat laziness or fatigue. It worked for me. My closest friend uses only positive affirmations to get that motivation and drive. No two people are alike. Determine which lines work best for you and consistently use them.

## Be Repetitive (playing mind games)

Repeat those lines—dozens of times each day if necessary—until they become second nature. Rehearse those lines like you mean it—as if you were an academy award-winning actor rehearsing for the movie role of a lifetime, which will propel your career to the next level. I refer to this process as *playing mind games.*

I accomplished more by the time I was 40 than most people have in two lifetimes. That may sound arrogant and egotistical but, I am not bragging, just proving a point. I am very humbled to be given the opportunity to be so productive. I am extremely proud of my accomplishments, structure and daily exercise regimen. Am I documenting these accomplishments to impress you? Absolutely not. My objective is to depict how living life with urgency can fulfil your existence. I attribute it *all* to God, living a healthy lifestyle and being disciplined.

## Most Frequently Used Excuses

How many times a week do you use lame excuses as a reason for not completing a goal on schedule or not keeping a commitment? In this section I've documented some of the *most frequently used excuses*. More importantly, I've documented the mind games I used to combat these excuses. The solution isn't rocket science. It's really quite simple, and may even seem corny, but there is a method to my madness, trust me! The solution is playing a mind game to train yourself to permanently erase excuses from your vocabulary.

## The "I Have a Cold so I Won't Exercise Today" Excuse

We've all been there. When you're feeling ill and your energy level is running on empty, it's easy to keep telling yourself that you should probably take it easy. Just about everyone else around you says the same thing. After a while you soften and ease up. The average person catches a cold twice a year. As you know, a cold can last anywhere from a day to several weeks, depending on the virus and severity. I've had my fair share of colds, especially being a parent with young children. They bring home the newest bug from school and share it equally among family members.

Granted, it's okay to take it easy when you're sick. However, as long as you don't have a fever, there is no reason to stay home from work or take a day off from exercise. It's important, though, to apply some common sense and consider the health of your co-workers, family and friends. There's nothing worse than the person who comes to work when they are ill and contagious. They're unproductive, but manage to infect the entire office as well as their families.

You won't have as much energy as you normally would, but you can still function. You're probably feeling a bit uncomfortable with a few aches and pains, but so what? What doesn't kill you will only make you stronger. It won't harm you. Why sit around doing nothing, complaining, and feeling sorry for yourself?

In the new millennium, no one has the luxury to sit around and do nothing. You're probably already doing the work of two people due to corporate layoffs, or because you have children and both parents are working. It's almost impossible to have extra hours for relaxation or personal downtime built into your busy schedule.

## Lines Used to Train the Mind

Train your mind by using lines to combat the *I have a cold so I won't exercise today* excuse. Below are some positive affirmations you may consider using:

- I will feel one hundred times better after I exercise.
- I'm tough and I can power through this.
- It will get my mind off how badly I feel.
- It may actually help me sleep better tonight.
- When I'm done, I can always come back to bed.
- If I go and exercise I will get my adrenalin going, get a good sweat and feel much better.
- The longer I stay in this bed, the worse I will feel.

Below are some negative lines you may consider using:

- Get out of bed and stop feeling sorry for yourself.

- You're pathetic if you stay in bed.
- Get out of bed and fight this bug—stop being a woose.

Get up and exercise a little; clean the house, or take a long walk. Just use some common sense and do things in moderation and don't over-exert yourself. The point is to keep moving. Then cool down a bit and take a shower or a relaxing warm bath. You'll feel so much better both mentally and physically. Use your favorite remedies, like chicken soup, tea, or medicine, and then get on with your day. Get up and stop wasting time hosting your own pity party. Make each minute of your life count.

When you catch a cold, tell yourself that you're not sick repeatedly, time and again. Reiterate in your mind that it's probably just a 24-hour bug. The more you accomplish today, the better off you'll be tomorrow. When tomorrow comes, it's more of the same, except now it's a 48-hour bug. You get the idea. Think positively. Don't wimp out here! Tell yourself it's only temporary and you'll feel better tomorrow. Give your body what it needs to kick this cold's ass! Take care of it and it will take care of you.

When I have those same nagging symptoms, people will ask me whether or not I am sick. My response has *always* been, "Nope!" The point is not to let people feel sorry for you. If they start pampering you then you'll start babying yourself. Don't go there—stay mentally tough! Always challenge yourself to push that much harder when you're feeling down. You'll be rewarded by significantly reducing your "down time" and feeling better sooner.

## The "I am a Busy Executive and Travel 80 per cent of the Time—I Don't Have Time to Exercise" Excuse

This excuse doesn't fly (pun intended) with me at all. I used to travel almost every week of the year. I was always in an airport and on the go. It's astonishing to see how many young executives in their twenties, thirties and forties are so out of shape. I hear the same old excuses:

- I'm always jet-lagged by the time I arrive at my destination and don't feel like exercising.
- I arrive at my hotel at an unreasonable hour.
- I don't have time—I need to get some work done on my computer when I get to the hotel room.
- I have to make some calls right now. I'll exercise tomorrow.
- I forgot to pack my workout clothes.
- I'm so tense from the trip, I need to get in the hot tub to relax my aching muscles.

And the list goes on...

What irks me is watching these flabby executives walk through the airport with their luggage on wheels. Many of them even have their smaller briefcases on wheels. To make matters worse, they take this wheeled luggage and stand on the automated walkways.

There are so many ways and opportunities to exercise before you even get on that plane. It would be wise to make it part of your routine, since you know you're going to be sitting for several hours. And let's not forget about all that processed rich food you'll probably be eating.

Some of the biggest excuses I've ever heard were from executives who complained how tired they were after traveling overseas. I'll have to admit international travel can be physically and mentally taxing. I frequently used to travel from Los Angeles to Singapore. I would depart Los Angeles around noon on Saturday and arrive in Singapore at midnight on Sunday. I can understand being tired, but so what? My mind would tell my body that I was tired just about every minute of the day if I allowed it to. Don't get me wrong, I get tired just like all humans do and I need rest just like anyone else—just not as much.

When you fly overseas, it's almost impossible to sleep more than a few hours due to the time difference. Singapore is sixteen hours ahead of Los Angeles. So why not get out of bed, turn the TV off and go to the hotel gym and exercise for thirty minutes? Most of the four and five star hotel gyms are open twenty-four hours a day. Once you complete your fitness routine you'll feel a hundred times better. What's thirty minutes? It's really not about being tired; it's just being lazy. Start walking at airports instead of using automated walkways. Forget the escalator; walk up the stairs to get your legs moving. Every little bit helps, especially when you have a long flight to take. These little things add up. Stop being so lazy!

## Lines Used to Help Train the Mind

Train your mind by using lines to combat the *I am a busy executive and travel 80 per cent of the time—I don't have time to exercise* excuse. Below are some positive affirmations to consider using:

- I will always exercise before getting on a plane. Even if it's an early morning flight. I will really exert myself. Who cares if I am tired—I will catch up on my beauty

sleep on the plane.
- If I exercise, I'll have the energy to take in the sights.
- Exercising will put me in the right frame of mind to attack my busy day head-on.
- What good is all the money I am making when I am living an unhealthy lifestyle by not exercising and not eating well!
- Exercising might help keep my mind off missing home.
- Exercising will help clear my mind and I will sleep better.

Below are some negative lines you may consider using:

- I am getting fatter and lazier each time I board that plane.
- I am going to die of a heart attack if I keep eating rich food, are overweight, and don't exercise consistently. Being a frequent flyer is no excuse.
- The way I look is up to me. Do I want to look like millions of other out-of-shape executives?

I kept telling myself that I was getting fatter and lazier each time I boarded that airplane. Before you go on a long flight remind yourself that you are going to be sitting for hours, and if you're in first or business class you'll probably be stuffing your face with rich food and most likely having a few drinks. If you workout in preparation for travel, you will feel better and be able to enjoy it knowing that you've taken care of your body first. You deserve to relax, enjoy the flight and indulge in whatever the food cart brings your way.

Everyone knows how a heavy meal alone can induce instantaneous napping. It's asking for trouble to combine inactivity with rich food and then adding a new timetable on top of it. Oh yeah, you're going to be feeling like crap for days. That's a shame since traveling can be much more rewarding if you are in good physical condition.

Another motivating factor for me is when people ask, "How do you stay in such good shape when you travel so much?" You never tire of getting compliments about your appearance because you know how much discipline it requires to stay in shape. The fact that people notice and acknowledge the difficulty in spite of my hectic traveling schedule shows that not only do they admire my commitment, but they realize that it's not easy by any means. More importantly, it proves that it can be done if you play mind games to keep your health a constant priority even in the face of adversity.

## The "I Can't Motivate Myself to Consistently Exercise" Excuse

During my travels around the world I visit dozens of new gyms each year. It's mind-boggling to see the dependency people have on personal trainers. There are so many people out there who will not exercise on their own. The reasons vary from being lazy to lack of drive or expertise, or solely as a status symbol.

I'm not condemning fitness experts. They need to make a living as well. Unfortunately, they oftentimes feed off these individuals who cannot motivate themselves. Lack of motivation is probably the number one reason people use them. It's sad but true.

If it's your first time exercising and you're not comfortable learning on your own, then I would recommend hiring a fitness consultant or personal trainer for several weeks. Most of them have the knowledge and expertise to show you the proper routines. It's important that you don't let the training sessions go on for more than a month. The sooner you become self-reliant, the better. Motivate yourself instead of being dependent on someone else. Periodic checkups to gauge progress or the lack of it is acceptable only if you feel it's absolutely necessary.

As most of you already know, it's hard to exercise consistently. Some days it's a real struggle and it's easy to find excuses.

There's always time to do some form of exercise. Excuses affect your health and quality of life. Here are some other excuses:

- I'll do it tomorrow.
- When I was younger I was much more consistent.
- Before I got married I used to be in great shape.
- I don't know the routine—I don't know where to begin...
- I don't feel very inspired today.
- I'm tired.
- I'm too busy.

I put this excuse last for a reason. Whether you're the CEO of a busy household or a corporation, there's always time to exercise. Make the time.

## Lines Used to Help Train the Mind

I played mind games as I was training myself to overcome some of those weak moments we all have. Not exercising consistently is a huge problem. Below are some positive affirmations you may try using:

- I will feel energized after I exercise.
- I want to make all of my exes jealous.
- I want to look great in my skinny jeans.
- It will help me de-stress.
- I'll never get the body I want if I don't exercise today.
- I need to exercise today because I'm worth it.
- Just do it!
- I'll feel awesome after I exercise.
- Each day I exercise the healthier I feel and the more energetic I become.
- I know it's hard to exercise but I can just imagine what fun it will be to show off in a size six dress at my reunion. (Visualize yourself in that dress, and how you'll feel when you're getting those looks of admiration.)
- I don't want to be ashamed of my body and scared of putting on a bathing suit, do I? I want to be proud of my body.

Below are some of the extremely (hardcore) negative lines I used:

- If I don't exercise today, I'll look like millions of other overweight and out-of-shape people.
- If I don't exercise today, I'll look like shit the rest of my life.
- If I don't exercise today, I'll become lazy and complacent.
- I'll feel like crap if I don't exercise today.
- I am a pathetic piece of **** if I can't motivate myself to exercise thirty minutes each day.
- I look awful—I wear clothes that hide my fat—even in the dead of summer—how long do I want to keep doing this?

- I look like s***
- If I take today off I'll want to take tomorrow off—this cycle will never stop—JUST GO DO IT.
- I am going to die sooner than later because I am obese.
- I'm a woose—do I want to be one for the rest of my life?
- I am a lazy slob.
- 'Push yourself, you loser.'
- Every day I take a break is another day wasted.
- How many days of being unproductive do I want to flush down the toilet?
- Scare yourself into thinking that If I take one day off I will end up taking another and another until it becomes a pattern.
- No pain, no gain!

These mind games seem outlandish, but they were mighty effective for me. I started using some of these in my teens and the rest of them in my twenties. Now in my elder years—they must have worked—I still exercise daily.

## The "I am Tired and Not Feeling Inspired Today" or "I Don't Feel Like it Today" Excuse

Maybe you were up most of the night partying and woke up feeling sluggish or, worse yet, hung-over. Perhaps you had a hard day at the office yesterday or maybe you're dealing with a lot of personal issues. Everyone needs to live it up and have some fun—and occasionally indulge. We should also be able to sleep in a bit. Having some fun is not an excuse for telling yourself you're tired today. Sure you can relax a bit and be lazy for a few hours, but that doesn't mean you need to take the entire day off and waste the day away. Save that luxury for a planned vacation so you can really enjoy yourself. Work hard now and play hard later.

It feels great to accomplish a major goal. The first reaction is to tell yourself you need to take a long break...and that's certainly warranted—heck, you deserve it. But some of you may not want a break—although your mind and body are telling you otherwise. If you want to keep charging forward, you may consider using some of the lines below.

## Lines Used to Train the Mind

Below are some of the lines(positive affirmations) you may consider using to combat the *I am tired and not feeling inspired today* or *I don't feel like it* excuse:

- Accomplishing a few goals feels great. When you accomplish, you're living, when you don't, you're just existing.
- If I take one break, I'll want to take more breaks. How badly do you want to leave behind a legacy? It's never going to happen if you take excessive time off.

For those of you who prefer using negative lines:

- It's stupid to take a break now—I'll take a VERY long break when I die!
- Although I completed one of my major goals on time, I failed because I didn't complete it ahead of schedule.

Being inspired can provide a worthwhile reason to get out of bed each day and to put that *snooze* button out of business once and for all. Do whatever works to *inspire yourself now*. It's very unfortunate, but it often takes a major life-changing event to shake most of us into inspiration. Creating your own inspiration is a significant life-changing event in itself.

## The "I am Overwhelmed and Feeling Stressed" Excuse

In the 21st century, feeling overwhelmed and stressed is a common occurrence. Your workload will continue to grow year after year. It's easy to shut down from circuit overload. Balancing your life will be even more difficult. Everyone tries to do too much. But doing too much is normal these days. God, family, relationships, work and exercise are all important. What is the right balance? Everyone is different, and there isn't one right answer. Everyone wants to live their own life and get as much squeezed into a day as possible. However, if you take on too much without your mind being trained to hold you accountable, it will surely lead to failure.

Develop your plan with the right combination of priorities. For me, it is *relationships, health* and *career*. Unfortunately, they're all a number one priority. Everything else has to be put on the back burner. Fun is classified as the bonus priority. If there is time, then so be it. Just in case you're wondering, there does happen to be time for fun, just not as frequent as some would like.

Once you have established your priorities, adhere to them. In your mind you must eat, breathe, and well, you know the rest of that phrase with your priorities. Don't take on any more than three priorities. The more you try, the more you will fail, and ultimately you will just get frustrated. It's important to get a taste of success early. You *never* want to fail, not even once. I despise this quote: "It's okay to fail as long as you try." If you keep failing, it becomes routine. Don't *ever* go there. Yes, you should always try, but tell yourself that failure is not an option. This will make you work that much harder to do your absolute best to avoid it, instead of telling yourself that "failure is okay". Always be afraid of failure. Continuous failure breeds more failure causing a lack of confidence and self-esteem. On the other hand, meeting ongoing success builds upon these important traits with each success, which spurs you on to a life full of successful endeavors.

## Lines Used to Train the Mind

Train your mind by using lines to combat the *I am overwhelmed and feeling stressed today* excuse. If you don't train your mind to think differently every time you're overwhelmed or stressed, you will want to take a day off. Below are examples of a few positive affirmations you may consider using:

- I will adhere to my to-do list and focus on one task at a time. Once I complete the first one, then I will take on the next one. It will feel great to continuously make progress.
- Once I meet my goal, I'll be able to relax, with peace of mind.
- It will be one less thing I have to do tomorrow.

Below are some negative lines you may consider using:

- Meeting my goals-scheduled completion date is a failure—I have to beat that date!
- I'm a loser and a failure if I can't beat that date.
- If I take one day off I'll want to take another and then another. I will always want a day off.
- Everyone is overwhelmed and stressed out these days. The world does not revolve around mre. I have to get

to it!

- Tell yourself, saying you're stressed is just an excuse—so what—go make it happen, you loser.

It may seem silly, but I would go out of my way to complete a goal way ahead of my scheduled completion date. This will also prevent procrastination. Always stay ahead of the game. You never know when you'll face an emergency.

Keep telling yourself that meeting a goal's completion date is not acceptable. I was training to automatically push myself every day to beat that deliverable. Call yourself every name in the book if that works for you. Do *whatever it takes* to beat that deliverable. You need to remember that it's *you against you*. Continuously challenge yourself and make it interesting so it's fun. It's like being in a sporting arena with your enemies as your goals. Beat them!

## The "I Can't Save Money and I Spend too Much" Excuse

You're not alone. Many people live from paycheck to paycheck. They struggle to keep up and never get ahead of the spending game. Their credit cards are usually maxed out and they pay only the minimum amount each month. They get so deep in debt that it's very difficult to resurface.

## Lines Used to Train the Mind

Train your mind by using lines to combat the *I can't save and I spend too much* excuse. If you don't learn to save and be frugal, you will always have financial problems. Use positive lines or directives like:

- Every time you go into a store, question everything you feel the urge to buy—even when you're at the grocery store. Most often you won't *need* it. Always question yourself several times with any purchase.
- Limit the amount of cash you carry in your purse or wallet. And if you're the type of person that has credit card debt, leave those cards at home. You can't spend what you don't have.
- Before walking up to the cash register, take out one or two items that you can live without for the next couple of weeks.
- Keep a good mental inventory of what you have stocked at home. This will keep you from buying items that you already have plenty of.
- If you have children, leave them at home when going grocery shopping. Ask them to write down what they need instead.
- When shopping for clothes, browse through the clearance and sales racks first.
- When you feel the urge to do impulse shopping, exercise instead.
- Leave your credit cards with the highest spending limits at home.
- If you are able to, pay off all credit balances at the end of the month.
- Don't spend on the little things; you will never be able to buy the big stuff (new car, home).
- Make a list of things you need, and don't buy any items that are not listed.
- Tell yourself repeatedly that you can save twelve dollars if you take your wife for the Saturday matinee show instead of the evening one. With the money you save

you can take her to a few nice dinners or buy her a nice gift. Always extrapolate re-occurring expenses throughout the year.

- Question yourself repeatedly. Do you really need to buy that item right now? You've survived without it all these years. The more you question yourself, the less likely you are to buy it, which means you probably didn't need it to begin with.

Deposit something into your account consistently and frequently. Preferably bi-monthly or monthly. If you have the option of depositing automatically through your company payroll deduction system, then do so. If that option is not available and you get paid bi-monthly then deposit funds into your savings account manually. You should also try to deposit extra funds, even if it's only a small amount. The key is to constantly watch your balance grow.

- Your mind will always want to look for more—but will never be satisfied.
- Eventually you will get bored at looking at the same number and will always force yourself to deposit more. It's a major sense of accomplishment to see that number increase frequently. The more frequent the better—your mind will be trained to anticipate a growing balance.
- Try and beat your own savings goals. Converse with yourself repeatedly, saying, "I NEED TO BEAT THAT NUMBER". Even if it's only by a few dollars.
- You can NEVER withdraw money from your savings account.
  - If you withdraw funds one time you will want to do it again and again. Have a hands-off policy. Your savings are only for major purchases (i.e. a house)

or for a major emergency (i.e. loss of employment).

Below are some negative lines you may want to use repeatedly until you've trained yourself:

- *I will lose my job any day now*. Although times may be good—it could change in a heartbeat—be prepared. This will force you to be cost-conscious throughout the year.
- I am broke.
- An emergency will happen for which I need to save. Emergencies are a fact of life. You're not being negative, you're being realistic.

Saving money and being frugal are sound financial management practices and should be your normal mode of operation. It can't be an afterthought. Unfortunately, millions of people don't save enough or have no savings at all. There are dozens of articles on the Internet exploiting the poor savings habits of people. Also, after facilitating hundreds of evaluations in my life coaching business, 90 per cent of my clients have minimal to no savings. They wait until they're in their thirties or even forties before they start thinking about saving money. This is a huge mistake they will regret for many years to come. They need to start learning about managing finances in their early teens. A solid foundation on the value of money should be initiated as soon as kids can grasp the concept. The more kids know about saving, the more likely it is that they will become financially responsible adults.

Who doesn't want a big savings account? Then all the more reason it needs to be a goal as early as possible. You must put future needs before present wants. Beginning is the hardest part. Once you begin, you'll never want to stop.

Making your own security blanket goes a long way towards lowering stress that can become a deterrent to completing even the easiest goals.

If your goal is to save one hundred dollars every month, then why not make a check out to your savings account just as if you were making a check out to pay your monthly bills? If you pay ten bills a month, what's one more? If you pay bills online then set it up for auto-payment right to your savings account. If one hundred is too much, then try fifty or even twenty dollars. It's important to set an achievable goal. If you're short on any given month, then you won't write this eleventh check. Tell yourself that it's just like any other bill and you're paying it on the first of every month. Remember to always pay yourself first and saving money will never be a problem. It must be a priority, plain and simple.

The savings account has to be out of sight and out of mind just like a safety deposit box would be. Don't open up another checking account, as you'll have a tendency to go to it when things get a bit tight. It has to be in *savings*. I had my regular checking account in one bank near my home and my savings in another, several miles away. Do not have easy access to your savings account!

The money in this savings account needs to be used to accomplish one of your goals, whether it's to purchase a car, a home or available for your children's education. Whatever you use it for, make sure it's for a significant goal and not for just a new watch, outfit or an impulse buy. Ideally, it should be for a goal that is something you need, but if it's for something that is just a want, then make sure it is well worth your efforts.

## The "I Have Too Many Problems to Worry about My Goals" Excuse

Personal problems or emergencies (i.e., divorce, death in the family, etc.) are the most difficult to deal with. Nothing can slow you down more than these types of heartaches. I've been through a divorce. Nothing was more painful and devastating, especially when children are involved. Mentally it can cripple you for a long time. It becomes extremely difficult to motivate yourself when you're going through these major personal problems. You just feel like digging a hole, sticking your head in it, and never coming up for air again.

Unfortunately, emergencies and personal problems can potentially knock you off your feet. Besides the mental anguish, there's the lack of motivation and emotional stress. Goals become an afterthought and you forget about work altogether. Sometimes severe trauma can put someone out of commission for a very long time.

## Lines Used to Help Train the Mind

Train your mind by using negative and/or positive lines and directives to combat the *I have too many personal problems to worry about my goals* excuse. Below are positive lines and directives:

- Dwelling on a problem that's out of my control is a total waste of resources. (Re-direct your energy into an outlet [i.e., your work, exercise, etc.] but don't sit there and dwell on the problem.)
- I can beat this feeling. (Tell this to yourself repeatedly.)
- I'm not the only one who has problems. There are

people in this world who are suffering far more than I am.

- The only one who can help me now is myself.
- I am stronger than I give myself credit for.
- I can do this. I am a survivor.
- This too shall pass.
- I may have lost the battle, but I can still win the war.
- I may be down but not for long.
- Tomorrow is a brand new day.
- Sometimes problems have a way of working themselves out.

Below are some negative lines you may consider using:

- Emergencies happen. I have to stop with the excuses already and get on with my life.
- Emergencies *will* come at the most inopportune time. I never want them to occur, but unfortunately they will—I have to be prepared. When setting a goal, I have to factor in emergencies.
- Failing to meet my goals' due date is unacceptable. Failure is intolerable.
- If I fail just one goal I will fail all of my goals. I am tired of being a failure. I will continue to be one for the rest of my life.
- I am running out of time.
- Next month I will be XX years old and I still keep pushing goals' due dates further out—this pattern will continue until the day I die. I need to change now.
- When I die, a picture will be placed on top of my casket and that will be the end of me. At the end of the ceremony, the only thing left will be that picture and memories. Leaving behind a legacy is just a pipe

dream—it will never become a reality. I have to make it happen.

- Meeting a goal's due date is failure. I need to beat that date—always beat the due date.

One of the comments I often hear is, "So what if I can't accomplish my goals on schedule? I have an excuse; it's an emergency." Missing a goal's scheduled due date is not good practice. If you do it once, odds are you'll repeat it. Training yourself to be prepared for an emergency will help you get over it that much quicker. After a while you'll be prepared if, God forbid, something does happen. You're trained, which will expedite your recovery time. Your mind will not let you veer off course. It's the whole idea of focusing on the positive things in your life to help you deal with the negative ones. This is why keeping busy is even more important when disaster strikes so you don't allow your mind to become consumed with only the stress or sadness you are experiencing. Life goes on and dwelling on painful situations just prolongs the healing process. Time doesn't heal all wounds, but it certainly helps if you allow it to by making the very best use of it no matter what.

## The "I am Always Late for Appointments" Excuse

This has got to be one of the most common problems people have all over the world. Reasons are endless, but the main culprit seems to be traffic. This is especially true if you live in a large metropolitan city. As I travel all over the world I see that traffic is definitely a problem, but being late for an appointment is no excuse.

## Lines Used to Help Train the Mind

Train your mind by using negative and/or positive lines or directives to combat the *I am always late for an appointment* excuse. Below are some positive lines you may considering using:

- The early bird gets the worm.
- If I'm late I will give a bad impression.
- I will draw attention to myself if I'm late.
- This is important to me so I have to be on time.
- If I miss this opportunity, it may never come again.
- I promised I would be there on time.
- I don't want to be known as the one who is habitually late.
- I will show poor character if I'm late.
- No one will trust me if I'm always late.
- There will always be traffic or an accident. I need to leave thirty minutes early.

Below are some negative lines you may want to use:

- Being late is disrespectful.
- Being late for any appointment is pathetic.
- There is NO excuse for being late.
- I am pathetic for always sitting in commute traffic because I can't get out of bed earlier. I have to get up and leave the house earlier since I don't have any parenting responsibilities. So what if I get there forty-five minutes early? It's better than potentially being late. I can sit in the car and do my work (make calls or get my tablet or laptop out), or while waiting for my appointment.

Also, if you always double your commute time, your odds of being late are slim. If you are chronically late and mind games don't work for you, then it's time to take it up a notch. Set all your clocks and watches twenty to thirty minutes fast. Before you leave your house, bring along reading material or your laptop just in case you reach there early. As I said earlier, time is money.

## The "I Can't Do It" Excuse

This has got to be the most exhausted excuse of them all. When things don't always go your way, they're the easiest four words to use in the English language. It's easier to give up than to keep trying to overcome a particular barrier. Do you want accomplishments? Do you want to be successful? Nothing worthwhile will come easy, whether it's that promotion or that special relationship you've always sought. *Just do it.*

## Lines Used to Help Train the Mind

Train your mind by using negative or positive lines to combat the *I can't do it* excuse. Below are some positive affirmations you may consider using:

- Tell yourself that you are smarter and stronger than you give yourself credit for.
- You'll never know what you're truly made of if you quit now.
- Tell yourself repeatedly that you can do it.
- Just do it.

Below are some negative lines you may want to use:

- Tell yourself that failure is not an option. Remind yourself that if you fail even once you will always lack confidence to take on new challenges. Saying "I can't do it" is the equivalent of failure.
- Are you going to be a loser and simply give up each time a new challenge comes along? Train yourself to be tough and to always persevere. Tell yourself repeatedly that you don't want to be a loser.

## The "I Can't Stick to My Diet" Excuse

It's not about dieting. Diets don't work for a prolonged period of time. You need to manage your health. That means eating right, exercising consistently and maintaining the proper body weight.

## Lines Used to Help Train the Mind

Train your mind by using lines to combat the *I can't stick to my diet* excuse. Below are some positive affirmations you may consider using:

- If I want to live long enough to enjoy the company of my children, grandchildren and great-grandchildren, I'll eat better.
- I need to set a good example for my children.
- If I don't take care of my health, no one else will.
- Having good health will make me a happier person.
- Having good health will make me more energetic.

Below are some negative lines you may consider using:

- Being fat is *not* beautiful, and it's certainly unhealthy. (Tell yourself repeatedly that fat is disgusting.)
- If I keep eating that crap I'm going to look like shit.
- Belly fat is not attractive.
- Flab is disgusting.

I always imagine what I would look like if I didn't eat right. When you are tempted to eat something that's not healthy, remember how terrible you always feel afterward. Your mind knows what's best for your body. You've just chosen to ignore it. So next time you eat that super-sized double cheeseburger meal you better check that mental snapshot. Focus on that mental picture and remember that you really are what you eat!

## The "I Need to Sleep a Few Extra Minutes—I Don't Want to Feel Tired Later in the Afternoon" Excuse

People have the most difficult time getting out of bed. Their minds will use all types of tricks to convince them to stay in bed for just a few more minutes. Your internal saboteur will throw everything at you to derail your progress—trying to keep you in that bed longer.

### Lines Used to Help Train the Mind

Train your mind by using lines to combat the *I Need to Sleep a Few Extra Minutes—I Don't Want to Feel Tired Later in the Afternoon* excuse. Below are some positive affirmations you may consider using:

- If I get up now I will have time to exercise and get ready for work properly. I don't have to stress about being late.

- I have a long to-do list. If I get an early start I can have more play time later.
- Another ten minutes add up to hours of wasted time for the year.
- If you're exhausted, another ten minutes of sleep will not help.
- If I lounge around in bed today I will do the same thing tomorrow and the next day.

Below are some ideas you may want to use:

- Stop lounging around in bed. Get up with a purpose and make something positive happen with your life.
- Be more productive with your pathetic life so you wake up with a purpose. Establish some realistic goals with daily milestones that will invigorate you.

If you're someone who has a difficult time getting out of bed when it's cold outside and uses the excuse "it's cold outside—I don't want to get out of this warm bed to exercise", do the following:

- Simplify your morning routine. Go to bed with your clean workout clothes on. It's much easier than having to get up and change into your workout clothes especially when it's cold or raining outside.
- Set multiple alarm clocks. Keep one of them far away from the bed so you will have to get up to turn it off.

## Treat Every Day Equally

How can every day be treated the same? What about holidays and weekends? It would be ludicrous to put forth the same effort seven days a week—everyone needs a break to recharge.

Besides, I'm not suggesting for you to be a machine seven days a week; just focus on your priorities first every day. Treating every day equally means doing a subset of your normal tasks and obligations on weekends that are associated with your priorities.

What if you don't want to do anything on Sundays but relax and watch TV? It's simple—just plan ahead and put a bit more effort into your priorities throughout the week or on Saturday. Don't just live your week by the seat of your pants—plan it out thoroughly. Be productive with your time and utilize every minute, so then you can feel totally free to goof-off and relax, or have fun.

Wake up thinking about your priorities first. That means, focus on your *career*, *health* and *relationships* at the start of each day, throughout the day and when you go to bed each evening. I consider these to be the most important priorities to live a successful life. The objective is to get into a routine, so focusing on your priorities becomes habitual (i.e., when you wake up, throughout the day and before you go to sleep).

Everyone says they want to live a balanced life; however, the only way to ensure balance is to focus on these three priorities *equally*. To accomplish this, you need to incorporate tasks, obligations and daily milestones into your routine and document them on your to-do list. I will discuss this in detail below.

You want to program your mind so that your actions help you achieve your goals. Eventually your mind will be trained and will be functioning as if it were on autopilot. I can hear the internal flack now: "That's utterly ridiculous; there's more to life than just thinking about your priorities" or "Does that mean I have to work all the time?" or "I can think about what I want to think about!" Or "I am tired and hurting;

why should I continue to torture my body? Maybe tomorrow."

These are all protests from your mind fighting the control. Your mind is used to having no control, sort of like a spoiled child. So, of course, it is going to give you a hard time and try to throw you off. All I'm saying to you is take control of your mind and harness that energy. Direct your energy into your daily milestones, which are associated with your goals, so that you are making progress every single day. The payoff will be that you will accomplish your goals. You are the captain of your ship. Just like we are sometimes stubborn about doing things that are not so healthy for us, we should be stubborn about committing to exercise. This is healthy, exciting, and in many instances, you make new friends.

It is your life, so you should control the direction in which it goes—take control of your life. Once you learn that you can achieve your goals, you are empowered to achieve higher and higher levels of success. Make sure those milestones get accomplished daily.

It is so easy to get overwhelmed with all the distractions that you can wind up going with the flow. However, the consequences of going with the flow and being pushed around by outside forces is that you never live your life, never accomplish your goals and end up feeling very dissatisfied. Below is a flowchart on how to treat every day equally.

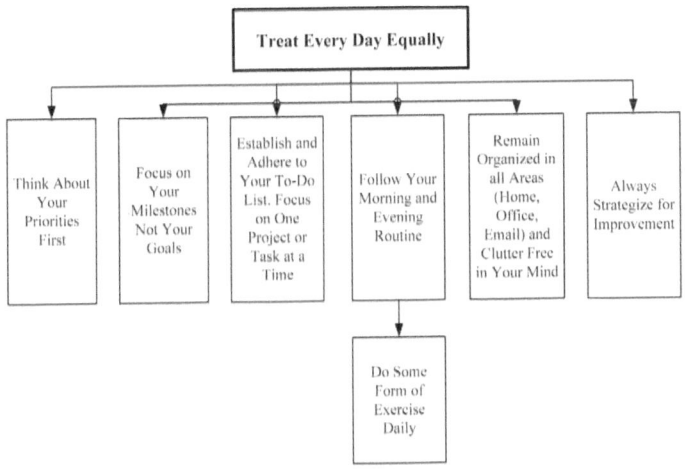

## Don't Set Goals...Yet

You may have reacted with surprise, skepticism and curiosity after reading the title for this section. You've probably heard on many occasions from many people, including self-help experts, that you should always set your goals first. Although just about everyone sets goals, the sad fact is that most people fail to accomplish them. Setting goals is easy. The hard part is thoroughly planning, establishing daily milestones, staying focused, being persistent and holding yourself accountable.

So what's the problem? First, many people think they're setting goals when they're really just dreaming. Dreaming involves aspiration; pursing goals requires perspiration. The reason most people don't accomplish their goals is that they're *unstructured*—disorganized; they don't follow a routine or adhere to a to-do list. Your goals need a solid foundation, and you get that when you institute structure into every aspect of your life. You can't possibly be effective if you have a mess around you and if your thoughts are distracted with clutter. You need to be organized *before* setting goals. Without structure you're setting yourself up for failure.

## Think Priorities and Focus on Your Milestones First

Wake up thinking about your priorities at the start of each day, throughout the day and when you go to bed each evening. The objective is to get into a routine so thinking about your priorities becomes habitual.

Goals planned properly should include milestones. Focus on these milestones—not your goals. Forget about your goals altogether. If you focus on your daily milestones and accomplish them, the goals take care of themselves.

I can hear the internal flack now: *That's utterly ridiculous; there's more to life than just thinking about your priorities,* or *Does that mean I have to work all the time?"* or *I can think about what I want to think about!*

Direct your resources into your daily milestones so that you're making progress on them every single day. The payoff will be that you accomplish your goals. You are the captain of your ship and it's entirely up to you to get it to sail smoothly.

It is so easy to get overwhelmed with all the distractions that you can wind up going with the flow and easily lose focus. However, the consequences of going with the flow and being pushed around by outside forces is that you never live your life, never accomplish your goals and end up feeling dissatisfied.

## Follow on Your To-do List

The only way to ensure that you are always focused on your

priorities to maintain that balance you seek is to document your daily activities on a to-do list. Use a simple to-do list to document and prioritize your daily activities (tasks, projects, family obligations, spiritual devotions and errands). Your to-do list should be written every evening or as the last task before leaving work—do not wait until the morning to document your activities. You need to hit the ground running in the morning—not wasting time by thinking of what to do next. Below are some helpful tips on how to effectively use a to-do list:

- Handwrite your tasks on a pad of paper and cross them off with a marker upon completion—you don't have to buy a fancy organizer to be organized. Keep it simple. Please, no organizers. I prefer using an 8.5 × 11 pad of paper and document all my to-do's in ink and cross things off as and when they are done with a marker. It feels awesome to cross off another activity with a marker.

- It should be next to you or in front of you 80 per cent of the time. Not on your desktop computer at home. If you prefer to have it on your iPhone or iPad, then look at that list frequently. I look at mine several dozen times a day. It's the only way to stay focused on your most important activities. Also, as you strategize (perhaps while waiting for a red light to change, or waiting for your doctor's appointment), write down notes—things to do in the future. Maintain your to-do list throughout the day. You will constantly be adding and deleting items.

- Prioritize your tasks. The unexpected always rears its ugly head and you may not get everything you want done on any given day. Carry the items that are not completed over to the next day.

- Remain consistent. The key success factor for the ultimate level of productivity is to consistently create and adhere to your to-do list. Establish a list seven days a week. Yes, even on the weekends, even if you only have household chores to do. Your weekend could have many more family and spouse-related activities like going to the beach or going out for dinner and a movie. If you do this *every* day for a few months it will become habitual and you will manage your time much more efficiently. You need to do this! The more efficient you are on the weekend the more time you will have for your family or just for relaxing. Once again the *only* way to maintain balance is to document all activities, including your personal and spiritual activities.

Preparing a to-do list may sound simple, but so many people have a hard time disciplining themselves to create one and follow it daily. Ensure balance and high level of productivity by following the tips above.

A to-do list should be prepared at the end of your workday or the evening before going to bed. Get in the habit of doing it when you complete your work on any given day. I do it before leaving my office. The last thing you should do is to create your to-do list for the next day. If you try to do it in the evening, you will forget more often than not or you'll be too exhausted to try and remember everything you need to accomplish. You want to be ultra productive each morning, not sitting there trying to remember what to do next. Have it with you wherever you go.

## Establish a Morning and Evening Routine

Treating every day equally means just that. Train yourself to be consistent by adhering to an efficient routine every day, which promotes your priorities. That doesn't mean all work and no play; it just means being efficient with your time so you can do more with less resources and still have plenty of extra time for play (however you define playtime). Do pretty much the same thing every day with some modifications (i.e., work emergency, weekend vs. weekday schedule, the days you have to pick up the kids from school vs. the days you don't, etc.).

## Don't Make Your Routine Complicated

Establish a simple routine. This is definitely where the KISS (Keep It Simple Stupid) principle falls into play. The more complicated it is, the more unlikely it is that you will use it for a prolonged period of time. You want to be able to memorize it, not write it down. If you have to write it down, then it's too complicated. An example of a simple morning routine could look like this:

- Wake up: 4:00 a.m.
  - Brush teeth, use bathroom, eat small snack and make coffee
- Morning ritual: 4:30 a.m.
  - Review Emails, drink coffee, say prayers
- Health ritual: 5:00 a.m.
  - Go to gym
- Pre-work ritual: 6:15 a.m.

○ Shower, dress and go to work

The evening routine should be just as simple:

- Dinner ritual: 6:00 p.m. – 7:30 p.m.
  ○ Prepare, eat and cleanup
- Next day preparation: 7:30 p.m. – 8:30 p.m.
  ○ Establish a to-do list (if you haven't done so already), pick out work clothes, make lunch, prepare work material and review Email
- Bedtime preparation: 8:30 p.m. – 9:30 p.m.
  ○ Meditation, reading, evening prayers
- Sleep: 10:00 p.m.

These are simple examples—yet they're effective morning and evening routines. Establish a morning and evening routine that makes sense for you.

## Exercise Every Day

Every routine should include daily exercise. Not twice a week or three times a week, but daily. I would consider everything listed below as exercise:

- Go to the gym a few days a week
- Go for a hike some day
- Wash the car once a week
- Walk around the block every other day
- Clean your apartment every other day, etc.
- Do sit-ups and push-ups every day

By exercising daily, therefore treating every day equally, you begin to maintain good health habits.

## Routinely Change Your Routine

Doing the exact same thing every day can make for a very dull life. Eventually, we all need change. Routines that keep you efficient are good, but occasionally change them a bit. Routinely change your routine. See yourself as an athlete who has reached a plateau, and in order to become better and stronger; he/she must change up their routine. It's not easy to change, because, as humans, we are definitely creatures of habit. The key is to adopt healthy, constructive habits, not unhealthy and self-destructive habits.

Try making small and subtle changes at first. Establish new milestones for your career, health and relationship goals. Think about adding some fun and excitement into your daily routine.

## Be Your Own Cop

You're the enforcer. It's difficult to be your own cop, but ask yourself this: *How badly do you want to be successful?* Practice being that tough cop until your mind is trained and it takes over those duties. If you break your rules, get annoyed. Be that drill sergeant insisting on excellence. A good analogy is when you have been driving for many hours, in many instances, speeding, and a police car appears in the rear view mirror. The natural reaction is to step on the brakes and slow down. If that police car never appears, you would probably keep on speeding. Being your own cop means enforcing your own laws, twenty-four hours a day, seven days a week.

## YOUR MIND IS TRAINED

Once your mind is trained, you will be in survival mode every day. You are trying to accomplish as much as possible before time expires. Every minute becomes precious.

- You will get out of bed each morning with a purpose.
- You will walk faster with determination.
- You will get to the point quickly and insist that others do so as well.
- If you're in management you will keep meetings short, to the point and focused on an agenda.
- Things that you procrastinated on for years will get done. You will have a *just do it* mentality.
- You will always be motivated and energetic to accomplish more—to always outdo your previous best.
- You will give yourself deadlines and not only meet them but *beat* them!
- You will operate with a sense of urgency every day.
- You will always hold yourself accountable.

Watch out world—don't slow me down!

## The End Result

Below is a flowchart depicting the end result—when your mind is trained to help you live like you're dying.

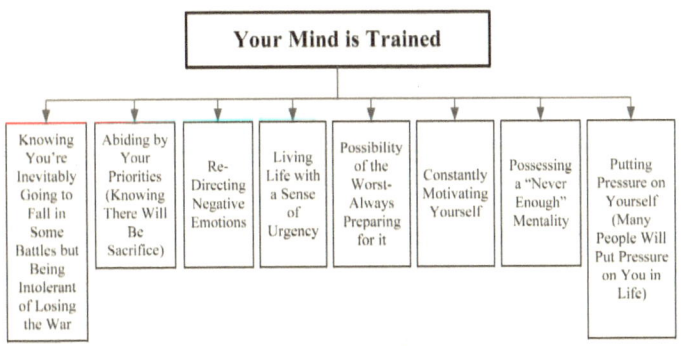

## Knowing You're Inevitably Going to Fall in Some Battles

Unfortunately, failure does occur at times, no matter how hard you plan and execute. If you do fail, you will be able to pick yourself up and push harder the next time around. You will also stop making excuses. So many times we blame others, our childhood, our boss, our wife. We get lazy or upset at a setback and then stop ourselves. If you fail a goal, you, and *only* you, are to blame!

## Being Intolerant of Losing the War

It may sound a bit extreme, but the more you've trained your mind that failure is the worst possible thing that can happen to you, the better your odds will be that failure will never be an option again. You will not accept excuses. If by chance you do fall, you will pick yourself up quickly and you will do whatever it takes to get back on course.

I trained myself to be so afraid of failure—calling myself

every name in the book you can think of in preparation for failure. Yes—in preparation for it because it's inevitable. *Right? Wrong!* You can never tell yourself that failure is acceptable, that it's just another one of life's little learning experiences. You must believe that failure is not acceptable or inevitable.

## Abiding by Your Priorities (Automatically)

You will eat, breathe and live by your priorities. The most critical priorities for success (for most individuals) are *career* (includes business, finances, education), *health* and *relationships* (God, spouse, business colleagues, friends). By the way, they're all No. 1 priorities. Obsess about adhering to them. Milestones and obligations associated with these priorities should be documented on your to-do list and achieved first. Train yourself to abide by these priorities first each day.

   Be persistent; distractions and obstacles invade your life every day. They get inside your mind and seek to make you forget your priorities. As soon as you let yourself be led by one of these distractions, you are no longer living Your Life.

## Re-direct Negative Emotions

How do you pick yourself up when you are emotionally down? One of the worst situations is when you get into a fight with your significant other. How many of you have lost countless hours of productivity because you were upset or depressed? Who hasn't gone through this scenario or through a breakup that's torn them apart and temporarily shut them down for a while? The worst thing you can do is dwell on it or sulk— it gets you nowhere. But that's easier said than done. When someone you care about so deeply was part of your life and then one day out of the blue you're alone, it's a lonely feeling.

Negative emotions can get in the way of completing your goals or just trying to concentrate on your job. In fact, it's one of the most common ways of stopping or slowing down progress. Many individuals go into seclusion when they're distraught. Based on hundreds of life coaching evaluations, two-thirds of my former clients would bury their heads in the sand like an ostrich.

Once your mind has been trained and you hold yourself accountable to your actions, you won't bury your head in the sand for countless days—you will fight back (not physically of course). You will redirect those negative emotions into your priorities and daily milestones.

You won't be able to turn off your frustrations and anger—don't even bother trying. You will stay angry but you will release your negative emotions into your work and into your exercise routine. It's a powerful force and you will use that force to work harder. You will be turning a negative into a positive by going into attack mode.

## Living Life with a Sense of Urgency

You will have an unquenchable appetite to continuously accomplish more, and the sooner, the better. You will do whatever it takes to accomplish your goals ahead of schedule. Just meeting a goal's due date will be unacceptable to you. Minutes become precious where most take them for granted. You value your limited resources. You're always strategizing to become more efficient with the resources you have. The objective is to do more in less time without compromising quality.

Most people would think this type of lifestyle is crazy—that you could never relax because all you're doing is worrying about completing goals faster or rushing through your daily errands and obligations. This seems very stressful. On the contrary, when you finish things ahead of schedule it's an unbelievable feeling and you will have more time to relax.

When your mind is trained to live life with a sense of urgency, you are conditioning it to constantly put pressure on yourself to do more with less. Your mind will NOT let up—it will keep that pressure on you day and night to produce more than ever before. You will accomplish your goals ahead of schedule. Once your mind is trained it won't matter what others try and throw on your plate—you'll always be one step ahead of them—bring it on.

## Possibility of the Worse—Always Preparing for It

S*** happens all the time, and most of it is out of your control. You can think positively all you want but in the end emergencies can happen anytime. When your mind is trained, you will prepare for everything. You will be a realist, but always hoping for the best. When establishing goals, you will always factor in emergencies. It's important not to miss a goal's due date and use the E word as an excuse.

## Constantly Motivating Yourself

When your mind is trained to continuously push you, look out. You will never need an alarm clock to wake up again. You will never need someone to push you to exercise. Although the project you're working on is boring, you will still push yourself to get it done as quickly as possible. You will never procrastinate again. It's like having a drill sergeant continuously barking out orders implanted in your head.

Accomplishments turn you on. The more the better. When are people going to realize that we're all on this planet for one time and one time *only*? There are no second chances. I can't imagine not accomplishing one goal after another (major and minor) until the day I drop. If there are no accomplishments, there is no life, or at best it's an unfulfilled life. There is no purpose for living. You may exist, but that's not living. Living is progressing, not merely breathing.

There is no greater feeling in the world than accomplishing a major goal. Once you complete a goal you will never forget it. It's hard to describe in mere words what the feeling is like. It's a kind of euphoria that not only makes you feel invincible, but is extremely addictive as well. The level of intensity is relative to the difficulty of the goal. The harder the goal, the stronger the "feeling of accomplishment" will be. You can take my word for it. I still remember each and every goal, even the ones I accomplished over forty years ago.

To me, life is about accomplishments and feeling on top of the world each time you've achieved one. What a rush, one after another, like no other feeling! Those are *real* highs. It's a self-inflicted adrenaline rush that you can't get out of your system once you've experienced it. The more you accomplish, the more you crave more accomplishments for yourself. You will *never* be satisfied. What a feeling it is to always want more and have that hunger to take on new challenges and to accomplish more year after year. Life now has purpose.

Once your mind is trained, you will always be motivated to accomplish more. You will be hooked.

## Possessing a Never-enough Mentality

*Never* being satisfied. The secret is to stay hungry. It's important not to become a workaholic in pursuit of your many accomplishments. No one lying on their deathbed regrets not having spent more time at work.

The true measure of a person's success and happiness is their emotional, physical and psychological well-being. Give thanks to the Lord for what you have and where you are emotionally, but never be satisfied with the level of happiness you've attained. There are always areas in our lives that need attention to keep the balance consistent. Being happy in all aspects of your life is the mother of all accomplishments. Once your mind is trained, you will never settle. If you must, remember to always settle for more.

## Putting Pressure on Yourself

Throughout life you're pressured, whether it was by your parents to get those school grades up, or to party with your friends you didn't necessarily want to hang around with, or your boss constantly throwing unrealistic project deadlines in your face, etc. Many times when the pressure comes unexpectedly, you scramble and become stressed to complete the project or assignment on time. Sometimes you can handle the pressure and other times you have a difficult time with it. Sometimes the stress is unbearable and you shut down.

You know it's going to come one day, so why not prepare for it. Why not condition your mind for the inevitable (i.e., emergencies that *will* happen, unrealistic deadlines that pop up out of nowhere, etc.). It happens all the time—you just don't know when... Your only recourse is to train your mind to complete everything before its due date so you have some cushion (resources) left over for the unexpected. In other words, constantly put pressure on yourself in order to be prepared for whatever is thrown your way. The pressures from the outside world will have no impact on you because you answer to yourself. I used the following lines to train my mind to put pressure on myself.

- Meeting my project's due date is failure. Beating my project due date is an accomplishment.
- I must ALWAYS be ahead of schedule.
- There are no excuses for missing a due date (not even emergencies). Emergencies should be factored into my timeline.
- You're going to die any day—hurry up and accomplish your goals.

These lines resonate with me, but everyone is different. Which lines will have an impact on your life?

## ADDITIONAL TIPS FOR TRAINING THE MIND

### Establish the True Underlying Reasons for Training Your Mind

Make no mistake about it—training the mind in order to achieve your goals is going to be one of the most difficult challenges you will face. This is why it's imperative that you identify the underlying reasons for taking on this daunting task. You'll have to dig deep within yourself and do some heavy-duty soul-searching to decide why you need to take this arduous journey of self-improvement. You are going to have to go into the deepest caverns of your mind and heart to figure out what you really want to accomplish in life. Once you have established what you want to achieve, write it down on a piece of paper and stash it in a secret hiding place for future reference.

## Ask Yourself: Is the Person I Truly Am Compatible with My Goals and Dreams?

Once you've mustered up the courage to acknowledge your goals and dreams, you must delve even deeper within yourself to determine whether or not they align with your character, physical and mental abilities. This is the ideal time to ask yourself: *Is the person I truly am compatible with my goals and dreams?* If there is any inkling of doubt, you will be destined to fail. Let's say you've always dreamt of being a world-class surgeon, but the sight of blood makes you squeamish or faint. What are the chances of you cutting into a living, breathing human being with a scalpel? What if you are being groomed to take over your family's business, which happens to be a funeral parlor, but you can't stand being around corpses?

The most successful people in life are the ones whose goals and dreams closely match their physical and mental strengths. So if you come to find out that perhaps you don't really have what it takes to excel in your chosen profession then come to grips with it and find out what you truly are passionate about. There is really no sense in selling your soul to Lucifer. You will never be happy if you have to compromise on who you truly are.

## Escape Your Comfort Zone

If you are one of those individuals who tends to shy away

from change at every turn, it's time to face your fear. You will not be able to master self-discipline or train your mind if you never get out of your comfort zone. There are different ways you can escape it, and here are some you might wish to try:

- You are sitting comfortably in a lobby when an elderly person or expectant mother comes in, and there is no other available seat. Be a good samaritan and give up your seat even if it means you might have to remain standing for a prolonged period.
- You are waiting in the check-out line at the supermarket with a shopping cart full of groceries. Another customer parks behind you with only a few items in their cart. Get out of your comfort zone by allowing them to go ahead of you.
- You've spent all day slaving in the kitchen. Now there is a sink full of dishes that need to be washed. Instead of leaving them sitting there overnight, get up and wash them now.
- The appointed time for you to exercise has arrived. But the mood is spoiled when you happen to notice that one of your all-time favorite movies is being aired on television. Instead of making yourself a bowl of popcorn, turn off the TV and hit the gym.
- If you normally take your morning coffee with sugar and creamer, try going an entire week without it or limit the amount you drink.
- You get an overwhelming urge to complain about something or criticize someone. Bite your tongue.
- You receive a call from a close friend professing to have some juicy gossip about someone you don't particularly care for. Resist the urge to gossip and change the subject.

## Meditate and Visualize Daily

If you wish to develop the brain power of a Buddhist monk, then you must take time out of your busy schedule to meditate and visualize daily. All you will need is a small, relaxing area where you can plant yourself and a few moments of peace and quiet. If you are a morning person, meditate and visualize bright and early while the members of your family are sleeping and you have the house to yourself. If you are more of a night owl, then meditation and visualization might be more beneficial to you before calling it a day and heading for bed. The fun part about meditating and visualizing is that there are no boundaries. It's your mind and you are allowed to go where you want, whether it's bathing al fresco underneath a beautiful waterfall, teeing off at a world-class signature golf course, or having a romantic candlelit dinner with the man or woman of your dreams. So go on and meditate and visualize your heart out and remember to reach for the stars.

## Make a Habit of Reading Personal Growth Material

In order for our bodies to thrive and be healthy, we need to provide it proper nourishment on a regular basis. If we fail, it's only a matter of time before our bodies will deteriorate and succumb to illness. Our brains require the same tender loving care. We need to fuel our minds by feeding it with new knowledge and positive reinforcement. One of the best ways to do this is to read self-help books. Since self-help and "how to" books abound in the marketplace today, you will have literally thousands to choose from. In fact, there will never be enough time to read everything that is available, so this is why you must choose wisely.

## Spice Up Your Life by Trying Something New

So many people today are content with living a dreary existence. They are close-minded when it comes to broadening their horizons. Instead of getting out of their comfort zone and trying new things, they hide behind what is safe and known. With the passing of time, their senses become numb and they stop growing as human beings. They do not let their spirits nor their minds soar to new heights. To keep your brain in good working order, it must have new sensory perceptions, experiences, emotions and knowledge to compute and process. Trying and experiencing new things is a sure-fire way to power up your brain and live a well-rounded and meaningful life. Here is a list of new things you can try.

- Learning a new language.
- Sample different types of cuisine.
- Befriend someone much older or younger than yourself.
- Listen to a new genre of music.
- Read a different genre of book.
- Try a new hobby.
- Order a tropical drink you've never tried before.
- Study a different culture.

## Maintain a Well-balanced Diet

Can you imagine what life would be like if we only had one food group?

With such an abundance of food available to you, there is no reason why you can't eat a well-balanced diet. Maintaining a well-balanced diet entails being self-disciplined. Without proper nutrition your body and mind will not work properly.

Eating a healthy breakfast is an excellent way to jumpstart your brain. If you have never been really big on eating breakfast, you will want to start with baby steps such as having a protein shake, a whole grain waffle or bagel, a small bowl of oatmeal, fresh fruit or yogurt with granola.

## Do the Horizontal Mambo More Often

While it's a well-known fact that love-making is one of the best ways to boost your immune system, studies have shown there may be a link between regular sex and improved brain performance, particularly in women. Doing the horizontal mambo with your significant other supposedly actually increases a woman's estrogen levels. Heightened estrogen levels can, in turn, result in better mental performance.

## Don't Skimp on Your Beauty Rest

Developing self-discipline and training your mind will be impossible to achieve if you don't get adequate sleep. Without sleep, your body will not be able to regenerate itself and you will slowly but surely start to lose your mind. Of course, you don't want to overdo the amount of time you spend snoozing like Rip Van Winkle did, but getting enough sleep can make a difference between mediocre and superior overall performance. Lack of sleep can easily interfere with your ability to assimilate information correctly and think rationally. It can also jeopardize your health and lead to a fatal accident. Ideally, you should be sleeping between the hours of 10:00 p.m. to 2:00 a.m., as sleep researchers have pinpointed this to be the timeframe in which the highest quality of REM sleep is experienced.

## Take a Trip Down Memory Lane

Dwelling on the past is a complete waste of time—or is it? Granted, everyone knows there are certain brain training games you can engage in to give your cognitive skills a boost, like completing a Sudoku or jigsaw puzzle. But did you know that recalling old memories can also give your mind a good work-out? Reminiscing about your glory days will allow you to tap into your memory banks. The further you go into your past, the more you will stir up the inner workings of your mind. Try recalling old memories during your meditation and visualization time.

## Be Good to Yourself

Training your mind so that it becomes a well-oiled machine is not for the faint of heart. The process will be downright painful and there will be times that you will want to be put out of your misery. Not everyone who begins this journey will get to the finish line. There will be some who do not have what it takes to master the self-discipline they need to achieve their goals and aspirations. If you are one of the few elite individuals who goes the distance and is able to train your mind successfully, then by all means reward yourself for your accomplishment. Only you can determine the best way to celebrate the realization of your goals. C'mon, be good to yourself, it is well-deserved.

## PART II

---

# HOW TO INSTILL A SENSE OF
# URGENCY IN OUR TEENS

# Parenting and Urgency with Children

If you are an adult fortunate enough to have a child in your life, then I'm sure you'll agree that he or she is a true blessing from God. Children are a special inheritance given us to protect and nurture. God is relying on us parents to educate and train our children by word and example because one day we will be held accountable for the inheritance that has been entrusted into our care. When that day comes, how will you have fared as a parent? Will you be able to look upon the inheritance you were given and see how it has grown and thrived because of your superior parenting skills? Or will your head drop in shame because you failed as a parent and squandered your inheritance?

Being a parent is a serious undertaking. We must shoulder a great deal of responsibility such as teaching our children to love God, honor their mother and father, respect the elderly, practice discipline, obedience, and undergo practical training for adult living. Not only do we have to instill all of these life lessons and principles in our children, but we have to race against the clock to get it all done in the nick of time, otherwise our inheritance will disappear before our very eyes. To keep this from happening, we need to instill a sense of urgency with our children, or their adult lives could be difficult. Many of you parents who are reading this book face tough challenges every day. It's a miracle you are able to keep your head above water considering your daily workload, errands and obligations.

These days children live a carefree existence and do not feel any sort of urgency. Only a select few are encouraged by their parents and mentors to *plan, set goals,* and establish critical *milestones* for their future, which starts when they turn eighteen. In the rare occasions that they are encouraged, it's done in a rather haphazard way. They have been reared to enjoy their childhood first. *They've got plenty of time to grow up.* How many times have you heard parents use that line? By no means am I implying that they should stop having fun altogether. Forcing them to bypass their childhood would be a travesty. Simply put, the youth of today needs to take a serious look at preparing for adulthood, which includes developing more than just scholastic skills. We spend our energy pontificating the importance of an education continuously, but how much effort actually goes into helping kids with their self-discipline skills, which is of equal significance if they are to grow into healthy, productive adults? You would do well to keep in mind that by the time your children leave home, they must be able to hold down their own fort in the following regards:

- They must have sound enough judgement to make wise choices and decisions.
- Be able to communicate effectively with others.
- Must be capable of taking care of their physical and mental well-being.
- Handle their personal finances wisely.
- Maintain and upkeep an apartment or home.

- Be self-driven and motivated without having you on the sideline to cheer them on.
- Recognize the importance of integrating spirituality into their daily lives.
- They must hold themselves accountable to their own actions.

Parents want the very best for their kids. There is no greater gift that you can pass on to your kids than being disciplined. It's a multifaceted and beautiful thing. First of all, it's an immediate reward in itself to see their face light up when they apply it for themselves and realize the impact it can have. Secondly, your life will be infinitely easier if you've developed your child's self-discipline from the start because everyone will be happier and well-adjusted. Third, you need to do it for society. What do you want to contribute to society? A happy, well-adjusted child that contributes to society or one that struggles at every turn? If you are not disciplined yourself then don't expect your kids to be. It doesn't mean that every disciplined parent will end up with a disciplined child. Each individual is built differently. If you want to give them every advantage in life, teaching them to be disciplined is the way to go. They have to be taught this ongoing lesson at every opportunity, but they have to be ready to learn it. Don't make the assumption that they will learn this stuff from others, because it's your responsibility, and the odds of that happening are pretty slim. It should come from you, but if another close family member or friend is willing, allow them to instill these ideas into their minds also over time. More role models are always better. They are watching and learning from you every minute.

## DON'T LET YOUR CHILDREN MAKE THE SAME MISTAKES

When it comes to our children, there are two things that most of us parents certainly do not want them to experience. Those of us who came from humble backgrounds are willing to do whatever it takes to make sure our children do not suffer like we did growing up. Even if it means working more than one job at a time and being absent from home frequently; we figure it's a small price to pay so that our children do not ever have to feel the sting of being poor or having to do without the material possessions that we were denied. Some of us overcompensate by spoiling our kids with expensive toys, electronic gadgets and designer clothing. We also pamper them by not assigning them responsibilities and household chores at home—heaven forbid they have to lift a finger. Many moms are notorious for waiting on their children hand-and-foot.

The second thing we do not want is for our children to make the same dumb mistakes we made on the road to becoming adults. As a parenting defense mechanism we take a strong hands-on approach in which we try to micromanage every aspect of their lives. As crazy as it seems, some parents actually try to relive their lives vicariously through their son or daughter. They attempt to dictate what sports their children should try, which college they should attend, and what their career choice should be. Some parents have been known to overstep their bounds by choosing the person their son and daughter should marry way in advance. Instead of raising our children to be independent and innovative thinkers for fear they are going to repeat our mistakes, we treat them like our own personal robots and try to program them.

As much as I hate to admit it, I have travelled a few miles down both of these roads before. Newsflash! Neither of these two parenting strategies work. Becoming your children's personal banker, indentured servant, or micro manager is clearly not the answer. Remember that your children have no idea what it's like to be a parent, so they are depending on you. Every decision, step and action you make as a parent influences how they will perform as parents. Without their parents shielding and pampering them, most kids will have a hard time making it on their own in every facet of life. The pressures to *do more with less* will only intensify as they exit their teen years. I can say this with certainty because many adults are struggling and barely surviving. Somewhere along the line, while growing up, their parents dropped the ball. The top issues related to the lack of discipline in their lives:

- Severe procrastination
- Poor financial management practices
- Failed goals
- No motivation
- No sense of urgency
- Lack of structure
  - Disorganized
  - Not following an efficient routine
  - Not establishing and following a to-do list
  - Not being punctual
- Poor sleep management

The top issues are enormous; if you're not proactive with your children's development now and help them acquire self-discipline skills, it will inhibit them from being successful—guaranteed! Just getting a college education alone is not enough. Yes, it's important to have a college degree, but it's only a small piece of the pie I refer to as *life*.

## GETTING BACK TO THE BASICS

Some of you may argue that being a father or mother in the twenty-first century presents unique challenges that our parents and grandparents did not face. All the new rules and society pressures makes raising our children much more difficult. For instance, according to today's society, you are not a good parent if you don't attend your children's school functions or you allow them to play in the street unsupervised. You are frowned upon as a parent if you don't enroll them in some kind of expensive organized sport or do their school projects for them. We are required to provide constant hands-on supervision even if it means missing work. The good ole' days when kids were allowed to venture out and explore life on their own, so long as they came home in time for supper, are gone for many.

Nowadays, the greatest enemy we face as parents is technology. Our children have so much information and entertainment available at their fingertips, making it difficult to compete for their attention. The youth of today are so engrossed in technology that they have completely become unplugged to their surroundings and home life. So what kind of modern-day parenting techniques can we turn to for help in the matter? *None! As* surprising as it may seem, today's parental challenges will require good ole' fashion solutions and getting back to the basics.

In Biblical times starting at the age of five, young boys were given training in agriculture. They were expected to help their fathers cultivate the fields and look after the family's livestock whether it was sheep or cattle. Some of them were even taught how to care for a vineyard so it yielded high-quality production. The idea was for the young boy to learn and perform the father's trade so that by the time he reached his own manhood, he would have the means to provide for a wife and children. On the flip side of the coin, girls were instructed in domestic arts by their mothers, which would be of great value to them when they entered womanhood. Teaching children the value of hard work at a tender age was and still continues to be necessary to forge them into productive adults. There is no reason for us parents to stray away from this time-tested parenting method, especially considering all the modern-day conveniences our children have access to.

Long ago, in an article in the *National Geographic*, I read about an eight-year-old African boy whose job was to get up at sunrise before everyone else in his household did for the purpose of fetching enough firewood for the family's daily use. In the heat of Africa, and barefoot, without missing a day, the boy had to walk close to ten miles for the firewood. After reading this article, it hit me like a ton of bricks. Making your child do household chores is not making them suffer. It's teaching them there is no free ride in life and they are going to have to pull their own weight. It's perfectly okay for them to make their own bed in the morning, do their own laundry, clean up their room, wash the dishes, or take out the trash. There is nothing wrong with making them leave their comfort zone for a while. You are doing a great disservice to your children if you expect nothing of them.

## LEAD BY EXAMPLE

Growing up, one of my greatest rivals was a snot-nosed, curly-haired boy named David. To say we despised each other is putting it mildly. We were physically sparring with each other every chance we got. I took some painful blows from him but I also dished out my fair share. One summer afternoon we were arguing about something in my backyard. Since we seemed to be getting nowhere in settling the matter, I bent over and scooped up a worm, which happened to be quietly inching its way out of our line of fire below us. With all the confidence in the world, I shoved it under his nose and commanded, "Eat the worm! If you do, then you win." At first Bobby looked at me like I had lost my mind, then a few seconds later a devilish grin spread across his face and he said something that immediately put me in my place. "You first!"

You simply can't expect kids to always do as you say if you don't have the self-discipline and motivation yourself to get the task done. In other words, you have to be willing to eat the worm first. It all starts with you. Nothing breeds discipline like discipline itself. Instilling discipline by showing and not telling first will help your children be successful. If you're efficient in managing every aspect of your life, your kids will take notice how productive you are. They may not say anything, but they're watching you. As they get older, they will mimic your behavior. On the other hand, if you live an unstructured lifestyle (disorganized and waste time) don't bother going into their messy room as they lay there on their bed playing video games for hours and ask them to tidy it up. They'll look at you as though you've just sprouted an extra head. There are many things you can do to showcase the importance of developing their self-discipline skills without cramming it down their throats:

- Get organized and maintain it.

- Be energetic, exercise consistently and be in good physical shape.
- Follow an efficient routine.
- Discuss career options frequently.
- Manage your household with a budget (be frugal and save).
- Don't waste time.
- Don't watch TV or surf the Internet aimlessly for several hours every day.
- Pray daily.

You are going to want to start with the basics and get organized at home. Keep your house, car and garage orderly. Chaos causes stress and prevents efficiency. If you are successful in this endeavor then you've earned the right to order your children to keep their rooms neat and tidy. But don't even dream of going there if your master bedroom and bathroom resembles a junkyard. The same goes for your working space. Make sure your office area is clutter-free, and keep your e-mail inbox manageable.

Remember that your children's eyes will be cast upon you at all times, so it's important to follow an efficient routine. Show them that you are in control of your life. Don't let time control you, and be structured throughout the day. This also means following a to-do list and letting your kids see that you maintain it throughout the day. Above all, exhibit good leadership skills. When you're in control of your hectic lifestyle and manage it effectively, your children will realize what a greater leader they have in you and are sure to follow in your footsteps.

## Teach Them to Treat Their Bodies like a Holy Temple

We each have been given but one physical body and it must last us from the cradle to the grave. Therefore we must treat it with self-love and respect, which implies nurturing it with healthy food, keeping it clean, exercising, avoiding sexual promiscuity, and not abusing it with drugs and alcohol. Our children must learn to appreciate their bodies, and it is up to us parents to make sure they take proper care of it. We can't expect for our kids to view their bodies as if it were a holy temple if we neglect our own. The best way to get this message across to them is by getting ourselves in shape, eating healthy and exercising regularly. If you're fat, lazy and have very little energy, there's a good chance that it may rub off on your children, and that's the last thing you want. There's no guarantee that just because you're in shape, they will be too, but it should improve the odds.

When it comes to doing their homework and exercising, kids need extra motivation. Many of them know that physical training is beneficial, yet they can't seem to muster up the enthusiasm to exercise. It may surprise you to know just how many pre-teens and teenagers actually fail their P.E. class. A popular line of reasoning among today's youth is, "Why should we get all sweaty and tired exercising when we could be inside our comfortable homes playing a video game?" Do you see what we are up against as parents? In addition to allowing them to see you break a sweat, you've got to remind them constantly that exercising has certain payoffs that is going to benefit them in the long run, and they are:

- Regular exercise boosts your immune system.
- Physical activity relieves stress and calms you down.

- Exercise and participating in outdoor activities makes your life more fun.
- Exercising consistently is easy on the eyes. Having a nice physique is a huge benefit.

Helping your children establish and maintain a regular exercise regimen is not enough. What good is it for them to exercise and train as if they are going to compete in the next Olympic Games if they continually stuff their faces with junk food? You can't expect your children to eat fruits and vegetables if they never see them on your plate. As tempting as it may be to go through the drive-up of a fast food restaurant for dinner especially after a long, hard day at work, sometimes the only way for your kids to eat healthy is for you to cook healthy. Your children also need to be reminded that eating fast food all the time is not the only way they can hurt their bodies. Pick an appropriate time and instill in them that smoking cigarettes, drinking alcohol and using recreational drugs cause serious harm to their health.

## WHY PUT OFF UNTIL TOMORROW WHAT YOU CAN DO TODAY?

We seem to have become a nation of habitual procrastinators. The No. 1 problem among adults and children alike is procrastination—putting off until tomorrow the things you should do today. It has been estimated that the average time wasted each day is four hours. Think about it—that's two months out of the year you can flush down the toilet. If you were to put your mind to it and extrapolate those wasted minutes, just think how much could be accomplished—it's a real eye-opener.

When my children were teenagers, every time I asked or reminded them to complete a task, I always seemed to get the same recorded message: "I'll do it tomorrow." The majority of children and teens today have a proven track record of always finishing their chores and homework assignments late. As a parent, have you ever asked yourself, "Why do my kids procrastinate so much?" The answer is rather simple. Children and teens procrastinate for the same exact reasons that adults do. Basically, there are four reasons:

- The task at hand seems overwhelming.
- They are extremely busy.
- Lack of motivation.
- The task at hand is boring.

So now that I've identified the top four culprits of procrastination, the question is, How do we help ourselves and our children conquer them? If the project or task set before you seems insurmountable, try breaking it up into individual steps until it becomes more manageable. Even if you are thrown off schedule, it will be easier to catch up by taking it one step at a time. Instead of wasting time dreading what you must do, jump right into the task cold turkey. Once you have determined that something needs to be done, start working on it right away. You can help your children by teaching them how to create a to-do list, and offer them tips on how they can organize their ideas and develop a well-thought-out plan for getting the job done.

Let's say that your child's main obstacle is getting his or her chores and homework done on time. How can you help them? This is going to require some creativity on your part, especially if the assignment your child must tackle seems boring to them. What you have to do is give them compelling reasons why they should actually beat their deadline. For example, you could say, "If you finish your homework ahead of schedule, the extra time left over can be used however you want." Remind them that they will have to deal with the consequences if they fail to complete their task on time. If they don't do what they are supposed to do in a timely manner, they will feel stressed out about it and their chances for success will be slim.

What if your child is already juggling too many tasks or activities? Is it cruel and unusual punishment to expect him or her to get their chores and homework done when they already have a full plate? Granted, these days children and teens do seem to be living life in the fast lane. Between home, school and all those extra-curricular activities, it's understandable that they feel overwhelmed and stressed. They are under a great deal of pressure. Teach them to tackle the easier tasks first. Get them started on tasks that are going to take them less than five minutes to complete, quick-hits like putting up their backpacks, hanging up their clothes, taking out the trash, or making a phone call. It is also important to show them how to correctly prioritize all the things they must get done. Have them create a list of their assignments and chores in the order of importance with a due date next to each item. There is a good chance that having them keep a schedule will make them feel as though they are in control of their time and they are likely to reduce their stress level. Finally, you will want to eliminate any distractions that could easily get in the way of them completing their tasks such as keeping video games, cell phones and anything else that goes *beep, beep or ping, ping* out of sight.

## DON'T BE AFRAID TO DISH OUT TOUGH LOVE WHEN NEEDED

Sometimes it takes a more direct approach to introduce adulthood priorities—I refer to it as tough love. Trying to *diplomatically* impart the importance of preparing for adulthood for most teens will be futile. After they finish with their schoolwork and chores, they want to hangout with their friends or play video games—right? That's perfectly fine. They do need to have some playtime to recharge their batteries. However, they also need to start planning for their future early in their teens, not when they're sixteen or seventeen. That's where parents can help by lending a slightly forceful yet helping hand.

In this era of trying to *do more with less,* you can no longer afford putting off the *mentoring* of your precious baby to survive, or better yet, excel in adulthood. Those golden teenage years are still wonderful, but being prepared for the next fifty years is more important. Yes, *much* more important. But where and how do you begin interjecting your wisdom? Your objective is to instill some discipline into their life without taking away their precious youth—but how?

A very effective method is to transform yourself into being a *nice asshole* and scaring them a bit. They need to know that being a teenager is a short-term endeavor, and some of it should be utilized for seriously planning their future. Scare them with the realities of being a responsible adult at the age of eighteen. Tell them that they have only a few years to be prepared for the real world and that their free ride will be over. Be brutally honest—don't sugar-coat the challenges of adulthood. It's much more difficult today than it was for parents over four decades ago. The pressures of *doing more with fewer resources* is enormous—they need to be prepared. End of story. *Please* don't gloss over the harsh realities of life. Our youth needs to start developing their self-discipline skills at an early age to be successful.

## RAISING YOUR CHILDREN TO HAVE SELF-DISCIPLINE

What does this mean exactly? Well, it doesn't mean punishing them physically. It means training them to become all that they can be without actually joining the military, being efficient with their time, and holding themselves accountable for their actions. Being disciplined will affect every aspect of your children's lives in a *very* positive manner.

One of the best places to start is by *instituting structure* into their lives. Get them organized, utilizing an efficient routine and using a to-do list every day. Teach them to be efficient and consistent. Mentor them to *treat every day equally* to *train their minds* to help hold themselves accountable for their own actions.

It's no secret that kids today squander an exorbitant amount of time. They need to understand just how precious time really is. Wasting approximately four hours a day is not all their fault. They had to have picked up this bad habit from somewhere, more than likely from *you* or another adult close to them. People mismanage their time mostly because they don't follow an efficient routine. They may try to, once in a while, but aren't consistent with it, or they don't focus on their daily milestones or to-do list. Mastering time is crucial for success in life. There's much more to do every day than there is time available.

Find the time to teach your children how to properly set goals, daily milestones and the importance of holding themselves accountable. Kids need to acquire and maintain self- discipline. Having good self-discipline skills will help them achieve goals for the rest of their lives. Self-discipline is the defining element in your life. With it you can achieve anything; without it you will struggle to exist. To learn more about acquiring self-discipline, read the book titled *Going from Undisciplined to Self-Mastery* published by Koehler Books.

## A PENNY SAVED IS A PENNY EARNED

Mentoring your children to have good financial discipline is probably the single most important area you can develop as a parent. Even if your family is well-off, being frugal in front of your kids will give them the right perception about finances. As soon as they start receiving an allowance, encourage them to handle their money wisely. Mentor them to *never purchase the small stuff—always save for the big stuff* (car and home).

Your children should know the importance of resisting the temptation to purchase the small, useless stuff and start saving for the bigger stuff that really does matter. If young adults have no clue how to effectively manage their money, it's just a matter of time before they get into severe debt, live paycheck to paycheck and have nothing to live on in their older years. They will go through much hardship in life.

Teach them to invest their money rather than spending it on things they'll stash in their closet and forget about tomorrow. That ability to save their money will help them obtain the things that truly matter in life. They should be taught as early as they start receiving an allowance that although it's theirs to do as they want with it, they are much better off saving it. Even if it means dropping what you are doing to drive them to the bank to make a deposit. Start training their mind early on that they have to start building their nest egg for the future right now. Mentor them on how much fun it is to watch your net worth grow every week.

Drilling it into your children's minds that when they turn eighteen they are going to have to start pulling their own weight (i.e., paying rent) may not seem like a nice thing for you to do as a parent. Unfortunately, it is a necessary evil considering that your kids are likely to start showing greater levels of maturity starting at the age of sixteen. This is about the time when they are going to need a car to get around in. No matter how tempting it may be for you—*please* don't buy them a car—*please don't do it.*

This way of thinking has nothing to do with trust. I trusted my daughter, but I taught her early in her teen years that being a teenager is a launching pad to adulthood. I repeatedly mentored her that when she turned eighteen, she needed to pull her own weight. She had to pay rent, purchase her own clothes and utilities unless of course she was planning on going to college. Those teen years is the time to be responsible, frugal, have a work hard mentality (with respect to school, chores and job) and live with urgency because you will wake up soon and you're legally an adult. If you don't mentor your children in their early teens, do you honestly think they'll be ready for the real world when they are eighteen?

While in high school, many of the students I went to school with, who came from wealthy families, were given new cars for their sixteenth birthday. I considered them the spoiled ones. A few (like me) worked several jobs and saved to buy their first car. It was apparent that kids who worked hard and spent their own money to buy a car appreciated it and valued it much more. I witnessed many of these rich kids abuse their expensive toys. As you get older, you appreciate your investments more from this tough love that was handed down.

You dads out there who have daughters know how hard it is to say no to your little girl. I am no different, but she needed to grow up in a hurry and earn her own keep. I kept telling her repeatedly at an early age, "Do not spend a dollar of your babysitting money, allowance and miscellaneous jobs. You will want/need a car when you turn sixteen." When she turned sixteen, she had enough money to purchase a good used car to get her back and forth to school and work.

You will send them the wrong message: that mommy and daddy will always be there to help you out if you succumb to the pressure of wanting to buy a car for your beloved son or daughter. You're causing more harm than good for their future. Let them earn, starting when they're in their early teens, and save, instead of purchasing songs online, buying a new case for their iPhone, spending money at the mall with friends or purchasing the latest keyboard on Amazon.

Some may argue, "Kids are not going to save enough money to buy a car doing odd jobs. That means that a kid would have to get a part-time job after school to get a car, and that means less time to study...bad formula, very bad." On the contrary, if they start saving their earnings in their *early* teens, they will have enough money for a good used car when they turn sixteen. Also, if you mentor them to adhere to their priorities (school), there won't be issues. Look at how much time kids waste playing video games, chatting with friends, watching TV, etc. Don't tell me that getting a part-time job will negatively affect their performance.

Every loving parent wants to buy a car for their son or daughter—don't go there. Instill a sense of urgency when it comes to saving money. Introduce sound financial management practices, self-discipline and priorities. If they know you're going to buy them a car, why should they save? That same thinking will be instilled in adulthood. They're going to come to you for assistance when it's time to purchase that first home.

Unless your family lives in NYC, where owning a means of transportation is not necessary, they will need a car pretty much everywhere else in the States. Let them hear it frequently—loud and clear, "I am not buying you a car when you turn sixteen." Repeat this over and over again, throughout their early teen years. It will eventually sink in. They should have been saving that allowance plus the money they've earned from odd jobs for the past several years—*if* you, as a parent, were mentoring them properly.

What about letting them buy the newest iPhone or hottest video game out in the marketplace? All of their friends are bound to have one. This is the ideal time to dish out some more of that tough love. They will always want the latest and greatest—who doesn't? As a parent it all comes down to you, and being that good role model. If you're always in the store pulling out your pocketbook buying whatever catches your eye, then you can be sure that your children are going to copycat you. This is something you can actually bank on.

In conclusion, your children are bound to learn sound financial practices, which they will need in their adulthood if you do the following: Create a budget for your household and stick to it. Use common sense and manage all three of these areas wisely:

- Expenditures
  - Don't spend frivolously.
  - Operate like you're broke.

○ Don't buy designer brands.

○ Don't be a compulsive buyer.

○ Don't buy on impulse.

○ Don't get into the car for every little thing. Consolidate your errands and obligations to save gas wherever possible.

○ Stay away from credit card debt under all circumstances. If you think you can't pay off your balance at the end of the month then don't purchase it.

○ When grocery shopping, look for sale items. Check the store's weekly flyers.

• Savings
Even if it's twenty bucks a week, save. The key is being consistent and keeping it all in the foreground, not burying it in your mind somewhere and talking about it occasionally.

• Investments
Be conservative and think long-term. Also, invest in property as soon as possible.

## HELPING YOUR CHILDREN NAVIGATE THE DANGERS OF TECHNOLOGY

Heart-breaking stories about teenagers who have died after playing extensive hours of video games are becoming more and more prevalent. As a mother of two teenagers, this really concerns me, and I can't help but ask if modern-day technology is actually killing our children. In July 2012, an eighteen-year-old Taiwanese male was found slumped over in his chair at an Internet café after having played a video game for forty non-stop hours without eating or sleeping. An autopsy performed on the teen boy revealed that he suffered a fatal blood clot after spending such a long time glued to his chair. The problem is getting so out-of-control that highly experienced psychologists and counselors who specialize in treating addictions are being called upon for "active duty." It's merely a matter of time before video game addiction is going to be classified and diagnosed as a psychological disorder alongside bipolar disorder, schizophrenia and mood disorders.

Studies have shown that those who have died from marathon-like playing sessions suffered from major blood clots. This is especially true of those individuals who already had a pre-existing heart condition. Other physical consequences include:

- Development of Carpal Tunnel Syndrome.
- Frequent migraine headaches.
- Insomnia and other sleep disturbances.
- Dry eye and other vision-related problems.
- Back pain.
- Eating irregularities.

Not only is technology posing a serious threat to your children's health—who knows what kind of psychological damage it is causing them? Some psychologists believe there is a strong link between video game addiction and aggressive behavior. The more violent the video game, the more it could actually desensitize your teenager when it comes to witnessing or learning of crimes committed against others. Then, on the other side of the spectrum, extreme video game addiction is causing depression amongst teens, not to mention doing a real number on their social skills.

What if your son or daughter is hooked on video games? How can you help them? Once again, it's up to you as a parent to lay down the gauntlet. You need to put a time limit on playing video games. Now, don't get me wrong, of course they are entitled to have some fun time after all, that homework can drain you just as easily as working a full day at the office. Everything within moderation. There needs to be balance— yes even as a teenager. Personally, I would limit video game playing up to one hour a day, especially on school nights. On the weekend, you could allow them slightly more time. Now let's say that your son or daughter is a video game addict. Is it reasonable to think you can actually succeed in getting them to stop cold turkey? Probably not! If this is the predicament you find yourself in, you are going to have to wean them off gradually, or else they are liable to self-combust from instant withdrawal. The trick here is that you are going to have to be creative in coming up with other activities. This could be the ideal time to get them involved with planning their future. Help them to set goals with key milestones, and more importantly, make sure you hold them accountable to those milestones. Finally, if you feel the problem is way out of your ability to solve, then consult with a licensed psychologist or counselor who specializes in treating all kinds of addictions. Consider the following early warning signs of video game addiction:

- Your child starts skipping school
- They have no interest in personal hygiene
- They grow distant from friends or stop socializing with others altogether
- Their grades start to decline
- Loss of interest in sporting activities they once enjoyed
- Poor social skills

## THE EXTRA CHALLENGES OF BEING A SINGLE PARENT

I've held many jobs in my day and I can honestly tell you that being a parent is by far the toughest, and most challenging. I can't imagine having to fly solo as a parent. Therefore, I have the utmost respect for single parents because they are extremely challenged and they have no one with whom to divide the parenting load. They have very little time to properly mentor their children. With limited resources, what are the most important things single parents can do to ensure that their children thrive in every aspect of their lives? By far the number one thing on that list is to *consistently* spend quality time with their children. Most of the time, being physically present for your children is the best medicine in the world for them. But since more than likely single parents are the designated bread winners, this is easier said than accomplished for the majority of them. Try your best to set aside at least thirty minutes a day, preferably more. The key is to be consistent so your child knows that they're always a priority in your life. Here are some other things you can do:

- Show that you care *every day*—be attentive when your kids are speaking.
- Even if you don't have thirty minutes a day, give them some time—success in any endeavor is all about consistency.
- Ask questions. Discuss school, friends, chores, finances, etc.
- Don't let them get lazy—make sure they're adhering to an efficient routine that balances between school, chores, future goals and play time.

One of the best things you can do as a single parent is to

have frequent heart-to-heart discussions about their finances and future career. Ask lots of questions—get them to start thinking about goals that are aligned under these priorities.

## Keeping the Lines of Communication Open

As much as it may pain you to speak to your children about direct and reality-filled subjects such as drinking, drugs and sex, it's absolutely necessary. Remaining mute on these topics is a huge mistake. If you don't broach these subjects with your kids, then count on someone else doing it for you. And trust me, this is the last thing you want. It's a dog-eat-dog world out there and the sooner your teenager can grasp this, the faster they will start preparing for the challenges ahead.

When it comes to keeping the lines of communication open with your children, the first thing you want to stress to them is that you operate on an open-door policy. Be sure you make them feel comfortable enough to approach you with *any* problem. Listen to them with a patient ear and always maintain a sunny disposition when they approach you. If you greet them with a scowl, then your children are not going to want to share their thoughts and concerns. As difficult as it may prove to be, do not overreact to whatever comes out of their mouths, no matter how shocking or unpleasant it may be. This takes a great deal of self-discipline and not every parent can pull it off.

Once in a while, you will need to patiently listen to some of their silly nonsense. Laughing at their jokes, listening to stories about their friends, and taking an interest in your children's trivial pursuits is sometimes the only way you can build a good rapport with them so that you can eventually go on to discuss matters of more pressing concern like finances and career opportunities and other topics of great importance.

## Make Your Kids Realize That Time Is of the Essence

Close your eyes and go back in time to when you were a teenager and had your whole life ahead of you. Now open your eyes and come to the grim realization at how quickly time has flown by. Can you honestly say that you accomplished each and every one of your goals? Of course not! Did you at least accomplish half of your goals? Probably not. As adults, we all have regrets about the things we were not able to accomplish, because time simply ran out on us. Do you want your children to have the same regrets when they get to be your age? It does not have to turn out this way for your children, but you have to help them realize just how quickly time flies by. If your children want to make all their goals and dreams come true, they must start living their lives with a sense of urgency fast and furiously. The more they accomplish, the more incentive they'll have to accomplish more throughout their life.

Remember, the guidance and wisdom you impart to your children now will someday be passed on to your grandchildren and great grandchildren. One day your children are going to become parents and will be accountable for their own children, their own inheritance. If you've done a good job with them, then chances are your children will do a phenomenal job caring for their inheritance as well, and the cycle of successful parenting will continue.

## DO IT FOR THE CHILDREN

Parents want the very best for their kids. There is no greater gift that you can pass on to your kids than discipline. It's a multifaceted and beautiful thing. First of all, it's an immediate reward in itself to see their face light up when they apply it for themselves and realize the impact it can have. Secondly, your life will be infinitely easier if you've disciplined your child from the start, because everyone will be happier and well-adjusted. Third, you need to do it for society. What do you want to contribute to society? A happy, well-adjusted child who contributes to society or one that struggles at every turn. If you are not disciplined yourself then don't expect your kids to be. It doesn't mean that every disciplined parent will end up with a disciplined child. Each individual is built differently. If you want to give them every advantage in life, teaching them discipline is the way to go. They have to be taught this ongoing lesson at every opportunity, but they have to be ready to learn it. Don't make the assumption that they will learn this stuff from others, because it's your responsibility, and the odds of that happening are pretty slim. It should come from you, but if another close family member or friend is willing, allow them to instill these ideas into their minds also over time. More role models are always better. They are watching and learning from you every minute.

AUTHOR CASE STUDY

# Professional Overview

The most frequently asked questions I receive have to do with my life coaching profession:

- What credentials do you have to be a life coach?
- What certifications do you have?
- How much experience do you have?
- What's your background?
- Can you help me get disciplined?
- I am a severe procrastinator—can you help me?
- I'm xx years old and I'm wasting my life away—can you help me?
- What makes you any different than the thousands of other individuals who claim to be a life coach?

The answers to these questions started approximately four decades ago for me. I was thirteen and what happened next was life-altering. It was a beautiful Saturday afternoon in the San Francisco Bay Area and I was cutting our front lawn grass. My neighbor Jim was outside working on his yard—as usual we just started bullshitting. Jim had a physique that Apollo might have wanted if the deity were actual flesh. He took one look at my skinny ass and told me point-blank, "you look like s***". The next Monday I started working out at his home-made gym three times a week. And so the mentoring began.

## WHAT A DIFFERENCE A MENTOR CAN MAKE IN YOUR LIFE

My neighbor taught me more than physical conditioning. I learned the importance of being organized, maintaining a good health regimen, strategizing about my future, focusing on my daily milestones, not my goals, motivating myself and treating my life with urgency. I also learned how to control my emotions by redirecting my negative feelings into positive acts or to drop the pain completely. Jim instilled discipline into my life. I may have been a little robotic until I grew up more and learned through life experience why we have emotions, especially the positive ones. But, the upside was achieving, on my own before the age of twenty, two milestones that few teenagers achieve: the first house (in the San Francisco Bay Area) and first brand new car (paid in cash).

I bring up the learning experience at the hands of my neighbor to bring home that while I may write several volumes about discipline that help people understand the concept, there is no substitute for learning from the right teacher. Humans need to learn from good teachers, because we aren't born with the means to defend ourselves or to contribute to the tribe. A baby is easy meat for any predator not kept at bay by either a bonfire or a twelve-tumbler deadbolt lock set into a solid block of oak.

As the child grows, the need for acquiring the gift of being disciplined and learning grows exponentially. We learn to feed ourselves by going shopping with mom and her fistful of coupons, or crazy Uncle Frank takes us into the woods and teaches us to sharpen sticks for use on the squirrels in the park. My neighbor was the more modern version of crazy Uncle Frank and I learned how to be a complete human being.

If I believe in healthy and positive mentoring relationships as being better than any old book, why did I write this and my other books on self-discipline? Well, good teachers can't reach everyone, and bad teachers abound, so the legacy I want to leave behind is that of books that teach the basics of the principles needed to survive a world with *five hundred channels and nothing on.* Or put another way, it helps for the teacher to have a book from which to *start* the discussion about self-discipline, or conjugating verbs.

## INFORMATION TECHNOLOGY (IT) CAREER

Approximately four decades ago, I took my disciplined mannerisms into the IT industry. The high-pressure deadlines, ultra-demanding users, constantly evolving technology and boundless opportunity were exhilarating to say the least, as long as you were disciplined. Here's how it started…

Two years prior to my eighteenth birthday I was researching industries that were going to be around for the long haul, be challenging and of course rewarding. Six months prior to my high school graduation I knew that I wanted to be working in the quickly-evolving technology field.

I was lucky enough to get my foot through the door in the Data Processing Department at GTE Lenkurt in San Carlos, CA (Silicon Valley). My job was to remove carbon from the reams of computer paper that were churned out by high speed printers housed in those glass rooms. Once carbon was removed, I had to burst and bind the paper for the various departments. I was paid just a little bit more than minimum wage.

My job was a blessing and now it was up to me to make something happen. I was rejoicing to be on the ground floor of the corporate technology department. Now that I was *in,* I wanted *out,* quickly. I wanted to climb the ranks as quickly as possible, acquire my experience and run my own IT department for a large corporation.

I finished my work-related responsibilities in four-to-five hours every day. I would then help out in other departments for the next five-to-ten hours a day. Management took notice that I was always there and helping out in three-to-four different departments within the organization. Yup, I was on the big guy's radar. His name was Warren Turtletaub, an intelligent Jewish man who was all business. He ran the IT organization. Most people in the department didn't like him because he was aggressive, demanding, possessed an even-keeled demeanor and he pushed hard. He would find out eventually that I was the same way—just a younger version.

I was promoted after five months; into the computer room as the graveyard computer room operator. I made one of my major goals come true. My congratulatory ceremony lasted five minutes. I wanted *more* and *faster.* To make a very lengthy story shorter, I continued to be promoted within the organization at the very least once a year.

At first my career evolved as a technologist, and after several promotions, I was at the top of my field as a Senior Systems Programmer. The pay was great but, again, I wanted more. To get *much* more meant to transition my career into management. I'll never forget the day I had my first management interview with Mr Turtletaub. As I mentioned, most people were afraid of him. I reveled in the opportunity to sit down with him.

He knew all about me and what I had accomplished to date. He said he was impressed but he also said to me, "What makes you think you can be a good manager?" I told him that I knew how to get the job done and I knew that no matter what—the job *must* get done. I was also very people-oriented. We quickly hit it off and I knew that he would promote me into his department's vacant management position—he did, one week later.

GTE Lenkurt closed its doors in 1982. Now to fast-forward my management career in IT, I took a leading role at Sun Microsystems' IT organization in 1988 (a multi-billion company responsible for hundreds of employees worldwide). I was their vice president of IT for the next sixteen years. I was responsible for the technology that ran the business. It was intense, stressful, and to say the least, extremely challenging. In my role, I was a full-time leader, visionary, politician, strategist, babysitter (yup) and mentor to staff. The business was always trying to do more with less, and so were we. It was a constant pressure-cooker. This was not an environment for the undisciplined or weak at heart.

I wasn't satisfied in just being a VP. I wanted *more* (gee, where have you heard that before...). We were the pioneers in technology. We had some major accomplishments at work and I wanted to let the world know about it. I quickly wrote a book in 1994 titled: *Rightsizing the New Enterprise,* and was published by Prentice Hall (PTR). After several weeks, it became a bestseller for them. The president of PTR called to congratulate me and asked when I could begin work on the next book. Book No. 2 titled *Managing the New Enterprise* was born. Then *Networking the New Enterprise* and finally *Building the New Enterprise* were released.

As if I didn't have enough going on already, the sales and marketing teams wanted me to facilitate customer talks, seminars and presentations to promote the company's services and products. In other words, I was on the road 80 per cent of the time promoting my books and the company's goods. I probably traveled around the globe four to five times and logged approximately four million miles.

You would think I would stop there, but I wanted *more* ... but not just another book. I wanted my own little publishing company—my own imprint (series of books with my name). I met with the executive editor of PTR in San Diego to present my plan. I wanted a series of IT management related books under the label of *Harris Kern's Enterprise Computing Institute*. Later that year we launched our first book in the series. After publishing approximately twenty books I retired the series in 2003. I then focused energy on writing books on the subject of self-discipline—I published five.

I kept being called on to fix, order and create discipline in the workplace. The light bulb went off and a side business was born. I mentored people and organizations using my neighbor's wisdom and what I had learned speaking to other successfully ordered people.

I thrived as a leader for thirty years and the key success factor was being disciplined. It certainly wasn't my scholastic background. I had a high school degree. What I had was much more powerful than a degree. My discipline instilled a sense of urgency and the confidence (chutzpah) to climb the corporate ladder as quickly as possible. My tenacity to learn things on my own was a winning formula.

## LIFE COACH AND ORGANIZATION PERFORMANCE MENTOR

Although I officially began my own business as a life coach and organization performance mentor in 2004, I've been helping people unofficially for decades prior to that. Helping people succeed was a *huge* turn-on for me, similar to what Jim did for me.

Matthew (fictitious name) was my pupil or subject if you will. When I first met Matthew, he was a loser. A bright, intelligent, and very personable individual, yet I still considered him a loser. He was going nowhere fast and needed some guidance in his life. This was a major challenge for me and a big one at that.

Matthew was a 35-year-old Operations Analyst at Sun Microsystems. I met Matthew in 1988 at Sun, when I was a manager working in the same organization, but in a different group.

Matthew was in horrible shape. He had gone through a divorce the year before. His wife fell in love with another man and had taken their only son to another state. His career was going nowhere; he had been given a written warning for poor performance at work, and he was on the verge of losing his job. Oops, I almost forgot: he was very thin due to eating no more than one meal a day. Yet no one could really blame him; as a matter of fact, we all felt sorry for him. His only outlet those days was partying at the local bars just about every night. Because of his good looks and great personality, Matthew had no problem meeting girls.

Matthew and I became very good friends. He would always be there for me. What I liked most about him was his honesty, sincerity and loyalty.

Outwardly, Matthew was a friendly and personable individual who would always go out of his way to help someone. I quickly hit it off with Matthew; he was, and still is, a genuinely wonderful human being. Yet, he was at a stage in his life where he was going nowhere.

When I first met Matthew, he held the most junior position within the entire data processing organization (computer operator). At our shop, much of the environment was automated, so that one could perform much of those duties while sleeping.

20 January 1993 was a weekday afternoon close to the end of the workday. I was walking into the computer room to speak with a colleague. I looked over, and there was Matthew on the telephone with a big smile on his face. You could tell he was talking to a girl. Probably one he had just met. As a matter of fact there were always girls calling for Matthew in the computer room. The scuttlebutt around the room was that anytime the phone rang, his fellow employees would say, "Oh, it's for you, Matthew." This was not the way one should be recognized at work. He had a perception that was anything but favorable. He had actually become the joke of the organization.

As I walked over towards him, something inside of me went off like an explosion (by this time we were pretty good friends). I asked him whom he was talking to, and he uttered some girl's name. It was not relevant, and I did not care what her name was. I told him to hang up. He could see that I was not kidding around. I had a very stern look on my face, and he could tell something was up. Within five seconds he hung up the phone.

He asked me what was the matter. "What time do you get off?" I asked.

"At five," he said.

I asked him to come see me in my office right after his shift. He said he had some personal things to take care of. I told him those things could wait; he was probably meeting some girl for a drink after work anyway. He said okay.

Matthew came into my office just after five and asked, "What's up?"

I replied, "Sit down."

Now remember, Matthew did not report to me, but, as a friend, I felt like he required some serious coaching. For the next three hours, I tore into him. There were moments when he actually broke down and cried.

"What are you doing with your life? Why are you throwing it all down the toilet? You are always complaining that you are overlooked for promotions, yet the perception in the computer room is that you put forth no effort to receive one." I added, "Do you think that someone will come and hand you that promotion on a silver platter?" My tone was stern throughout this entire conversation. "Do you like working at this company?"

He replied, "Yes," but every computer operator's dream is to be promoted out of the computer room and into a much more challenging and better paying job. He wanted out as well, but he did not know how to change things around.

Right about then I felt like kicking him in the rear end and said, "I cannot believe you have been a computer operator for the past seven years." I gave him a stern look and added, "Matthew, let me tell you where you are. Go buy a gun and point it at your head and fire, because you might as well be dead. You are a damn loser and failure."

He was shocked, but he did not argue. I told him that he was going nowhere quickly. He agreed with me. I said to him, "From this day forward things are going to change! This is your last opportunity in life." I knew he was listening. This also became a goal for me, and you know what that means. I wanted to see if *discipline* could make a difference in someone else's life. The only drawback was that Matthew had neither drive nor initiative, so I was doubtful he could acquire discipline, but I knew I would help turn his life around.

"Things *will* change. I am tired of listening to you whine about your current position and status. You *need* to help yourself!" At this point Matthew was very distraught. He asked what he needed to do. "Work is now the priority—your only priority!"

I was extremely rough on Matthew, never letting up on him, not even for a moment. I will never forget when he actually broke down and cried. It hurt me as well, but it had to be. "Effective immediately," I said, "you will have a contract with yourself. You will adhere to the following rules and guidelines."

1. You will not accept any non-urgent personal phone calls during working hours. The only phone calls you can accept will be from family members, yet those will be limited to one a day. You will tell them (in a nice way, of course) no more phone calls unless it is an urgent matter that needs to be addressed immediately.

2. You will put in extra hours every day. Ask your supervisor for special projects. Starting tomorrow, you will no longer leave work at exactly five. There will be no more clock-watching. You will put in an extra one or two hours each day to start with. "But," he said to me, "I'm an hourly employee and won't get

paid for those extra hours."

I said, "Yup!" It is like donating your body to charity. "You are going to make some wholesale sacrifices in your life."

3. We will sit down together and determine your next career move. Then you will have a discussion with your supervisor to advise him that, from this day forward, your life and career are changing. Based on your past performance, your management will probably not take you seriously, but that is okay. They know, just as I know, that anyone can talk—the hard part is performing. In addition, it is just as important to sustain that performance year after year.

4. Start training and studying for that next position. You might need to take some night courses, purchase books, or train with senior staff. Whatever the requirements for that next position are—you will gladly meet them!

5. There will be no more dating until you achieve your goal. (I knew this one would kill him because he was such a ladies man). You will be working on projects and studying for that next position. No excuses whatsoever. You will not have a personal life until we turn this around.

6. You will provide me a weekly status report on your progress. That report will be due in to me every Monday morning by 8 sharp! Matthew replied, "But, Harris, my work shift doesn't begin until 9."

I said, "Very good, my little buddy, you're starting to get the hang of how this works.

Failure to comply with any of the above at any time means I

am through mentoring you. You can continue to be a loser. I will still be your friend, but I will not waste my time.

There are no guarantees this will work. Let's see if we can turn that perception around with some constructive results." The goal for Matthew was to get his act together and become a productive employee. A promotion would signify success.

"Oh yes, one more *very* important piece to this puzzle: you need to *want* to do this. I cannot force you to do this."

He thought about it for about a moment. Suddenly, it became very quiet in my office. "I really want to do this," he said emphatically.

"Are you sure?" I asked again. "This will be the most difficult and stressful ordeal you could possibly go through, next to your divorce. You will hate me at times. I take that back, you will probably hate me all the time, *until* the day you receive your promotion." I told him that this would be a dramatic change in his lifestyle. It would be difficult for him (or anyone else, for that matter) to go through this ordeal. "Now tell me, but before you respond, sit in here for thirty minutes and think about it."

I started to leave my office at 8 that night. He was alone. "Oh, by the way," speaking as I was walking out, "I will not be angry if you say 'No.' This will not affect our friendship one way or another." It was important for him to know that, and more importantly, to have it out there. I did not want to force anyone into doing something they did not want to. I just knew that Matthew needed help, the right plan (strategy and roadmap) and a big push; there was no way he could do it on his own.

When I returned, Matthew was sitting there quietly. "Okay, bud, what will it be?"

"Yes," he replied.

"Are you sure?"

"*Yes!*"

"Matthew, I am asking you one more time. It is okay to say no. I will still value our friendship, *but* if you quit halfway through this ordeal, I will be very disgusted with you."

Over the next year and a half, Matthew changed in a big way. Not only did he abide by the guidelines I set for him, but he also attended night school to acquire some applicable skills. To top that off, he never went out on a single date during the entire period. Don't worry, he started dating again, but only when he was ready. He had become a very different person. He was beaming with confidence. He understood the power of discipline and the positive effect it can have.

By the way, I almost forgot to mention... Matthew was promoted out of the computer room! Then, a pleasant surprise: he was promoted again. He was promoted twice within three years. What makes me any different than the thousands of other individuals who claim to be a life coach? *I walk the talk.*

- I was mentored at a young age and practised what I learned throughout my life.
- I am highly accomplished in Information Technology (consulted with hundreds of Fortune 500 and Global 2000 Companies, traveled the globe several times and pioneered the newest technologies).
- I have mentored hundreds of individuals and organizations.
- I have exercised every day for more than four decades now.
- I have an extensive leadership background (thirty-plus years in corporations and small business)
- I have written over forty books

- I purchased a brand new car at the age of sixteen (paid in cash and insurance)
- I purchased my first home in California at age nineteen.
- My car and boat were featured on the front cover of Hot Rod magazine (July 1975 issue) at age twenty-one.

What is life all about? Leaving a legacy behind for my family and for others who could use a little discipline in their life!

# Early Childhood

My parents were a great influence on me. They worked tirelessly and managed their money wisely. My mom worked eight hours a day reupholstering furniture, and then transitioned to her second job which was raising my brother and me. She was an incredible woman with a giant heart, the size of Mount Everest, and an abundance of energy, however, not to be outdone by my father who worked sixteen-hour days washing dishes in an upscale restaurant. His only goal was to make sure we always had food on the table, nice clothes to wear, and a roof over our heads.

My mother had an extremely difficult upbringing. She was born a Jew in Damascus, Syria. Being Jewish in a country that was, and remains, hostile toward Jews was challenging to say the least. They were segregated in certain areas of the country and never enjoyed the taste of freedom. When my mom was eight years old, a decision was made by the local elders where she lived to flee with as many Jewish children as possible over the Golan Heights into Israel to be free in a democratic society. The adventure began in the middle of the night. With very little and practically the clothes on their back they walked for countless miles through treacherous terrain without making a sound over the Golan Heights into Israel and for the first time in their young lives, these children, my mother included, got to savor the sweet taste of freedom.

My dad's childhood was also full of heartbreak and adversity. He grew up without parents as they were both killed during the Holocaust by the Nazis. By the skin of his teeth, he was able to escape death, but his ordeal left him with permanent scars that never did heal. He was raised by a very mean lady who fed her biological children first. If there happened to be any leftovers, they were given to my father. He never complained—he was grateful to have a roof over his head. He never really spoke about the trials and tribulations he was forced to endure as a child or an adult. My mother found out about the hardships he suffered through his brother, and she eventually told me. My dad is now in his eighties, and until this day, he still refuses to talk about it.

As the story goes, my father migrated to the U.S. by himself during the 1960s with just enough money to survive for a few months. We had relatives in Kansas City, Missouri and Los Altos, California. He was (and still is) a proud man and never dreamed of asking for any kind of handout. Although our relatives in Palo Alto were extremely wealthy, he never asked for help. Just like so many others who heard about this great country called the United States of America; with its abundance of opportunity, he wanted us to have a shot at a better quality of life.

My father and mother met in Israel and were married. My brother and I were born there. He eventually saved enough money to fly all three of us to the U.S. in 1960. I had never seen the inside of an airplane up close before—now I was in one heading straight for America. I clearly remember how excited I was—I could hardly sit still—playing with the overhead buttons and lights.

When we moved into our first apartment in San Francisco we didn't have much money, but our household was a loving one. Our apartment was situated directly across from the ocean. The area was okay. It was a far cry from Shangri La but it wasn't anywhere near the worst part of the city either. We made a lot of good memories growing up, but there were also a few awful experiences that got permanently seared into our minds. One of the most awful childhood moments I can remember occurred when I was seven years old. I recall leaving the apartment complex one morning with my mom and we happened to stumble upon a dead body—someone had been murdered. That must have been the most negative incident of my young life. Well, on second thoughts, I take that back; there were also neighborhood bullies who terrorized my days. They would occasionally take my lunch money. If I didn't pay up they wouldn't let me cross the street so I could get to school. They were bigger and a few years older than I was. Luckily, most of the time we took our lunch to school—they had no need for that.

At the start of the sixth grade, we moved to San Mateo, California, which was about a thirty minute drive south of San Francisco. It was a typical middle-class community. It proved to be a really challenging time for me because the bullying was much more severe. I was tall and lanky with zits all over my face. My nickname was crater face. The kids were downright brutal. Whether it was during classes, before or after school, they had a real knack for making me feel worthless.

The problem was much more than just my face being full of zits. I was pathetically skinny—about as scrawny as you can imagine; six foot tall and one hundred thirty-five pounds. I was a real pushover; it didn't take much for bullies or any strong gust of wind to knock me over. I tried my hand at sports to try and fit in. I attempted to play soccer, football, baseball and basketball but I had no athletic ability whatsoever...no team wanted to pick me.

As for school, I knew I had to graduate, but I didn't like attending classes. I thought many of the subjects being taught were useless. After graduating from junior high school, I really had no direction in life. I was just another kid floundering around aimlessly in a deep ocean. To summarize:

I was a scrawny thirteen-year-old kid growing up in a typical middle-class neighborhood. I was that kid the neighborhood bullies loved to pick on:

- I was riddled with pimples
- I felt like I had a lower than average IQ.
- I was uncoordinated, with no athletic ability to speak of. Actually, when it was time to pick teams for PE activities, I was always the last one chosen whether it was for baseball, tennis, basketball. It didn't matter which activity it was. I was always the kid no one wanted on their team. In retrospect, it was a truly degrading ordeal for me.
- I couldn't swim to save my life. When it was time to engage in water activities, I always made excuses not to participate.
- I had no muscle tone whatsoever, and was the typical all-rround weakling.
- I had a short attention span. My brain never stopped strategizing. Staying focused through my high school classes was almost impossible. Nope, I didn't have ADHD—I was antsy to get out and make it on my own. I felt the classes they were teaching (History, Government, English, Geometry) were irrelevant and wouldn't play a role in my future. So I did the bare

minimum to get my diploma. As hard as I tried to be attentive and learn these subjects, I couldn't do it. I felt they were irrelevant to real world experiences. Only a few made any sense to me.

I had no confidence in any of my abilities. My confidence level was at an all-time low. I felt like a total loser.

## MY MENTOR

My neighbor Jim Jarman was in his forties when he made a deep impact on my life at age thirteen. Talk about a male specimen: intelligent, handsome, sincere, with a great physique, hard worker, good family man and a great personality to match. I always looked up to him.

On one of those typical warm summer California days, Jim was outside, mowing the lawn, shirtless. We would always be clowning around together, trading sarcasm punches. On this particular day, he said the five magic words to me that changed my life forever: "Harris, you look like shit." As you can imagine, we were pretty good friends.

I could tell immediately that he was serious. He was right; I knew it. At the time, I stood six feet two inches tall and weighed one hundred forty pounds (after a very large meal). If I turned sideways, you wouldn't be able to see me. I was that skinny. It was a disgusting sight!

I looked at Jim and said that I knew it, but genuinely did not know what to do about it. I ate everything in sight but could never gain a pound.

"Harris," he said, "eating massive amounts of junk food is not the way to approach your problem. Your mind and body need a major overhaul, and it doesn't start with your mouth."

At thirteen, I did not understand what he was trying to tell me. How else do you gain weight?

"If you decide to follow my instructions to the letter then I will help you out." I said sure, not having a clue as to what was forthcoming.

"I want you here every Monday, Wednesday and Friday after school. What time do you usually get home?"

"I get home at 3 every day," I replied.

"Okay, on those three days, I want you at my house by 3:15, and don't be a minute late. If you're late, the deal is off—no second chances." This was Saturday, so we started on Monday.

I was really looking forward to my first session. Maybe, just maybe, I could obtain a body like his in no time and my life would change for the better. What a rude awakening! He put me through hell! To say it was a very stern exercise program is putting it mildly. It turned out to be three days a week of torture, always pushing me harder than the week before. There was weight training, running, swimming (he taught me how to swim), and most importantly, lecturing me as we were exercising. He would always keep me focused on the exercise and our long-term objective. It was continuous badgering. There was no time or place for social talk.

Jim also went on to teach me not to rely on anyone for help. Why not? Is it not okay to rely on your friends occasionally? Not for acquiring discipline to accomplish your goals. It is 100 per cent you and no one else. Athletes know that 80 per cent is upstairs (in the mind), where it all starts, especially on those days that you're too tired, stressed out, or simply not in the mood--that's when you need to push yourself the most. He was training my mind more than my body, although I did not know it at the time.

Jim was like a drill sergeant. But the whole time, he was instilling me with discipline. I figured if he was willing to give up his precious time to help me out, the least I could do was show up on time. Besides, after I agreed to do this, he actually dared me to quit or show up late. He tested me during each and every one of our training sessions.

Looking back now, I realize what an illusory mind game this entire ordeal was. His tactics were highly effective, scaring me into never being late. I did not know it back then, but he was training my mind, starting with the easiest form of discipline: punctuality.

# Ages Thirteen to Nineteen

## MONEY DIDN'T GROW ON TREES FOR US

We didn't have designer clothes or shoes to brag about or show off. There was no fancy china to take out when we had guests for dinner. My brother and I were given a modest allowance for duties performed around the house and outside, mostly general cleanup work and washing the car. My parents typically said no to special purchases, especially if it was the latest and greatest widget we saw on TV. If I wanted something that wasn't school-related, then I would have to purchase it myself. They taught me not to spend my money. Dad and mom kept telling me over and over and over again to save, save, save for the big stuff. This was continuously pounded into us. My parents worked extremely hard for every dollar, and they saved most of it and spent only on the bare necessities of life (rent, food, clothes, healthcare, etc.).

Right before my Bar mitzvah, my dad wanted to stress a very important point since I was two years older than my brother. "Soon you will be on a path toward manhood. The training period is relatively short. You have five years to take full responsibility and ownership of your life. Once you turn eighteen, you become a legal adult and there's no turning back. At that time, I expect you to pay for rent, purchase your own clothes and help pay for food. When you turn sixteen, you'll probably need to buy a car and pay for your insurance." I will never forget that stern look he had on his face. That look coupled with his low and clear voice was enough to send shivers down my spine.

My father knew perfectly well that the US was different from Israel in many ways. Yes, the good old US was the "land of milk and honey" and that's why everyone wanted to come to this beautiful country. In his mind, it was also a country where many adults became successful and then they would get a bit lazy when it came to raising their children. It was much easier to spoil their children than to instill discipline into their lives. These days most parents say yes to just about everything their children want. This is a formula for disaster. Dad wanted to make sure that my brother and I were not spoiled and we would be able to make it on our own.

When my father spoke, he got right down to the nitty-gritty, and never sugar-coated anything. I remember one day he said to me, "If you get into any sort of trouble with the law, I will ensure the police takes your ass to jail. You will sit there and rot. I won't come to bail you out." Those were his exact words. It's been forty-seven years, and those words are engraved in me permanently until the day I die. He knew how to scare me to the point that I avoided all situations that could potentially get me into trouble. Putting that fear into me had a *deeply* profound impact.

My dad meant it when he told me, "*You will pay rent when you turn eighteen, and you will not drive my car when you turn sixteen, and get your license. I will teach you how to drive with it, but you will need to buy your own car just like I did.*"

I knew that I had to make it on my own, and that was fine with me. And I had to start earning and saving money quickly.

## AGE THIRTEEN: ENTERING THE WORKFORCE

Right after my Bar mitzvah, I started asking all of my neighbors for any sort of work. It didn't matter who offered me work and for what amount; I took what I could get. I wasn't shy about asking for work. I never really bothered to ask how much the job paid. I'd happily accept whatever number they threw at me. At this age it was about working and making money. No job was too big or too small; I performed whatever work came my way.

Can you imagine a thirteen-year-old *boy* babysitting? In the 1960's, it was considered normal for a girl to babysit, but certainly not a *male teenager*. I was watching over my neighbor's two young children almost every Friday and Saturday night, making fifty cents an hour. I earned approximately five dollars a night—in 1967 that wasn't bad money. As quickly as I made the money, I deposited it into my savings account. Even if I only babysat one evening and made five dollars for the entire weekend, I would still deposit it into the bank.

I was mentored early in my childhood that it was critical to save for a rainy day. It was exciting to watch your bank numbers grow. I learned to always save, and avoid withdrawing unless it was for a major investment like a house. Each new savings-related milestone I reached was exciting to see. Eventually, the numbers began to multiply. My first fifty dollars turned into one hundred, and then five hundred. In those days bank books were issued—I loved getting that bank book stamped with a new higher number each week.

The biggest challenge during my teen years was dealing with the peer pressure. Most of my schoolmates in the neighborhood were hanging out on Friday and Saturday nights at this park near my house, typically doing nothing but bullshitting, smoking cigarettes and pot. Some of them were even drinking beer heavily. As you can imagine, I was ridiculed profusely for not joining in the so-called festivities. To me it was a complete waste of time. I'd rather be working and making a quick buck.

- My neighbor across the street owned a travel agency. His name was Mel. One day I asked him if there was anything I could do for him at his travel agency. If I remember correctly, the name of his agency was called Melcoh Travel. I doubt there are any more of these brick-and-mortar agencies left, since booking a trip is all done online now. In response to my question, Mel said to me, "There are travel brochures you can file." I went to work for him every Saturday morning, and he paid me seventy-five cents an hour. I did filing and general cleanup work.
- For a time, I worked at an automobile junkyard, removing batteries from old broken-down cars for a dollar twenty-five an hour. I hated this job with a vengeance. I would come home dirty and all cut up every night. As you can imagine, a junkyard was an unpleasant environment. Occasionally, you would even see some fairly large snakes, and I wasn't a big fan of rattlesnakes then, or now. One time, as I was unscrewing a few bolts to pull a battery from a car, I heard a rattlesnakes —there was a large one living in this clunker—it was the last time I pulled a battery.
- I worked at my local gym for a few hours on the weekend, mostly making protein shakes and picking up the weights. I was paid a dollar an hour, but one of the fringe benefits was that I got to workout for free!

- On the weekends, I did yard work, which involved pulling weeds and mowing lawns. I accepted whatever people wanted to pay me. I didn't have a set price.
- I delivered newspapers on Sunday mornings and was paid thirty-five dollars a month.
- I washed cars of all shapes and sizes and took whatever amount people wanted to pay me. I reasoned I was getting my exercise while making some spare change.

Sound financial management practice is key to having a better life. The advice my mentors gave me became my motto: Save, save, and save some more. Save every coin, every dollar. Throughout my childhood and adult life, priorities were fairly simple. Back then, I referred to them as *money*, *gym* and *sex*. What can I say—I was a real stickler for simplifying things. The proper and politically correct way to identify these priorities are *career*, *health* and *relationships*. Once again in my defense, I was a teenager who classified priorities in my own special way.

## Money Makes the World Go Round

It's sad to say this, but without money, it is difficult to survive. This world, more than ever, revolves around money. It's the foundation to success and happiness. Money isn't everything; it's made out to be, we all know that, but if you develop sound financial discipline, you can focus more of your energies (with less stress) on your relationships (God, family and business colleagues), not to mention your health. I learned a few simple concepts in my early teenage years, and those same principles still apply today:

- Don't spend what you don't have. Don't act like our

government.

- Don't borrow from your friends or family. They have their own bills to pay. Don't depend on others.
- Deposit as much as you can in the bank as frequently as possible.
- Never withdraw from your savings account—unless it's for a home or a car. Vacations don't count. If you're someone who likes to take frequent vacations then have a separate account especially designated for that purpose.
- Rent is a bad four-letter word—you should purchase a home as soon as possible.
- Keep your checking and savings accounts separate.
- Save *big-time* for emergencies—they will happen.
- Don't overspend on non-essentials. Spending on music paraphernalia is not essential. My friends used to spend their allowances on the latest and greatest eight-track tapes or cassettes each week. Ironically, people and their bad spending habits haven't changed all that much. One of my clients downloads dozens of songs at ninety-nine cents a pop. He also spends substantially on video games.
- Never impulse-buy. If something you think you need catches your eye, but you're not quite sure, then surely you can live without it. When in doubt, walk out of the store without pulling out your wallet. Adopt a *never enough mentality* when it comes to earning. Strive to always earn more.
- Every penny still counts—never walk past a coin. Don't be lazy; bend down and pick it up—when you get home put it in a jar designated for coins only.
- Don't spend on the little things, and eventually you'll

have enough save*d to spend on the bigger* things.
- Don't lend money to your friends. There's a high probability that you'll never see it again, and your friendship will be destroyed in the process.
- Have several different sources of income. Don't keep all your eggs in one basket.
- Forgo the designer brands.

These concepts may sound rudimentary, but they're highly effective. These were the principles I followed throughout my life and they made me financially secure by the time I was thirty-eight. Nothing has changed. I still follow these principles religiously.

## Pumping Iron for Confidence

The first day of weight training for me started in one of Jim's spare bedrooms. He had some old barbells and dumbbells, among other home-made exercise equipment. He also built a wooden bench press out of 2x4 boards and some rug for padding to work our pectoral muscles. We started out by using his new bench press. He started me out with light weight on the first set. We did two more sets with a bit more weight added after each set. After that we did a few more chest exercises using some of his old dumbbells.

We would typically do chest, shoulders, back and finally biceps and triceps. Jim was very patient—he was teaching me the importance of good form versus the actual weight in the beginning. We also ran sprints to strengthen my legs. We were exercising three times a week consistently and over time it was apparent that the stronger I became the more confident I was.

Jim eventually showed me how to train my mind.

Although I didn't know that's what he was doing at the time. He taught me to use lines that would have an impact on me. Lines that made me react in a very aggressive manner to always push myself harder. Just like when he was mentoring me—I jumped when he barked. The first lines I chose were the same ones Jim used on me from day one. I also picked a few others:

- I look like shit!
- I'm a loser!
- I'm a woose!
- Just do it!
- Hurry up, you're wasting precious minutes!
- How long do you want to look like this?

These were my all-time favorites. I repeated these lines everyday—pretty soon my mind started pushing me harder and harder. Over time my body changed—I actually had strength, and my confidence level was growing to a sky-high level.

## AGE SIXTEEN: BUYING MY FIRST SPANKING BRAND NEW SET OF WHEELS IN CASH

Aaah, turning sweet sixteen—for many kids it was pretty much the same activities, studying, partying, dating, hanging out with friends for hours on end. Sure, there were a few responsibilities to deal with, like doing homework, chores, studying, and perhaps working at a part-time job. Teens whose parents were well off had fewer responsibilities than the rest of us.

I was already into the third year of being productive with my time. I was going to school, working and saving as much as possible. I was taught to remain organized, to follow a to-do list seven days a week and establish and stick to an efficient routine. For me, it was all about making money, exercising daily, and, in my spare time, having fun with girls. In that order, I might add. I used to refer to these priorities as *money*, *gym* and *sex*. For me, it was always about my priorities. Nothing interfered with them. Those priorities came first—everything else had to take a backseat. Were they the right priorities? At this stage of my existence, I had no clue, but it was working for now.

The time came for me to buy a car, a junker, so I could learn how to drive and get my driver's license. I didn't want to practice on whatever new car I would eventually purchase. I also wanted something to get me back and forth to work. I paid $75 for an old Volkswagen Beetle that leaked about a quart of oil every week. It was downright ugly—but I didn't care. It was good on gas and I didn't have to spend any time cleaning it. It met my needs. My mom, dad and friends couldn't believe that I would even drive this ugly duckling of a car. I didn't care. My eye was focused on the bigger picture. That bigger picture was my dream car. After a few months it was time for me to buy something special.

Most of the car dealerships near my home were in Burlingame, California, which was approximately fifteen minutes north of us. One weekend I asked my dad to go car shopping with me. We drove down the auto row and within minutes I saw the car of my dreams. It was a shiny maroon-colored '69 Chevrolet Chevelle SS with a black vinyl top and beautiful chrome rims. You could spot those shiny tires a block away. We pulled over and walked onto the dealership lot. As soon as we got to the car, the salesman came out to greet us—like a great white shark waiting for his next victim. He opened the car doors so I could sit inside while my dad checked out the engine. The car was stunning.

My dad went inside with the salesman and did all the negotiating—I just waited outside. After about ninety minutes, my dad came out jingling the keys in his hand. He had made out a check and I reimbursed him with cash when we got home. I don't remember what I paid for it. It didn't matter—it was my dream car.

I drove it home. The car went in the garage. My dad's car remained outside. Shortly after we got home, we ate some lunch and I went into the garage to wax it. My dad used to wax his car every few months—I used to help him. He made it a point to teach my brother and me the importance of taking care of our most prized possessions.

I drove it around to school and work for a few months. That old Volkswagen Bug remained out on that street corner. All of a sudden the kids around the neighborhood who were always ridiculing me now wanted to be best friends with me. It seemed like overnight I went from everyone's joke to the hero of the neighborhood.

## AGE SEVENTEEN: ASSEMBLING THE CAR OF MY DREAMS AND REINVENTING MYSELF

One day I went to a classic and muscle car show at the Cow Palace in the San Francisco Bay Area. Wow—these were the crème de la crème of cars. I was impressed by the intricate detailing that went into these cars and motorcycles. Spectators of all ages were ranting and raving down every row of cars. There must have been hundreds of the most beautiful machines ever assembled. They were all incredible—that was a bit of a problem for me—there wasn't one entry that stood out from the pack. I knew that I wanted my car exhibited here one day under the lights. I yearned for more—I wanted better. I wanted something truly special. I didn't want just another fancy car. I wanted something that would stand out from the crowd. I couldn't exactly pinpoint what I wanted yet, so I started small.

The first thing I wanted to do was get several car parts chrome-plated. I started with the glove box, rear differential cover and the centre console. In those days cars were made with more steel than plastic. Once those parts came back from the metal shop, I put them back on the car that evening and I quickly became addicted. I wanted to get everything chrome-plated—and so the transformation began. During a one-year period, my friends and I took everything that could be removed easily and had it chromed.

I also installed a chromed tube axle to replace the underside of the front-end and a chromed deep-dish oil pan. There was chrome everywhere including the rear-end and drive shaft. It was a sight to behold. When I drove that maroon beauty down the street, people couldn't believe their eyes. But still, it wasn't enough. This was becoming a pattern with me in every aspect of life. It wasn't only the car. It was my workouts, my earning power, saving power. I felt like I was invincible—I had the discipline to conquer the world—it was all there for the taking.

You could say I was different than any other teenager. I was confident, focused and always on a mission. What had happened to me? I was disciplined and I was no longer in control. At this point my disciplined mannerisms controlled me. While my friends and schoolmates were always thinking about partying, I was *always* strategizing on how to achieve the next big goal faster and more efficiently. I was very robotic and extremely focused on my daily milestones to get to the next big accomplishment in my life.

I was hungry for more success—constantly craving more, and wanting it yesterday. The next thing I conquered had to be bigger or better than the previous goal. I couldn't believe how, in just a few short years, with the help of my neighbor and parents, I was transformed from having these characteristics:

- Being weak
- Lacking in confidence
- Scrawny
- Not focused on anything of substance
- Lacking direction

to having the following characteristics:

- Goal-oriented
- Confident
- Results-oriented
- Physically fit
- Strong
- Efficient
- Focused
- Constantly motivated

Yes indeed—life had a major purpose for me at such a young age.

## AGE EIGHTEEN: STARTING TO CLIMB THE CORPORATE LADDER

One year prior to A-Day (18th birthday—Adulthood), I began researching different career opportunities. I also researched many companies in the San Francisco Bay Area where I lived. I wanted to understand the corporate climate, and which

businesses would be around for years to come in good times
and bad. You can't predict which companies will survive bad
economic times, but you can try to improve your odds by
picking one that's been around for a few years. I also wanted
to know which particular industry would be thriving and
be considered a business enabler to change our corporate
landscape for many decades to come. The answer was
Information Technology, although back then it was referred
to as Data Processing. It didn't take me long to decide that
technology was going to change the world. And boy, has it
ever!

I was eighteen years old, fresh after graduating from
high school and hungry to land my first corporate job. I
was fortunate enough to get my foot in the door of GTE
Lenkurt's (now Verizon) Data Processing Department in San
Carlos, California. In the seventies, I knew that computers
were not only here to stay, but they would eventually manage
all businesses, small and large.

My job, as I said, was to take the carbon out of the paper
when it came off the printer. The position was that of a burster/
decollator. Once I removed the carbon, I would separate the
reports based on department names. It was a simple yet *very*
dirty job. Can you imagine removing carbon from paper for
eight hours non-stop? I couldn't. I was able to get my job done
in approximately five hours, which then gave me free reign
of the department. I befriended other department heads and
asked to help out in their areas. My goal was to get promoted
to another department within Data Processing as quickly as
possible. I knew exactly where I wanted to go. I wanted to get
into the computer room to run the big mainframe computers.
But to get there I had to work in other areas and prove myself
first. The first area they referred to as the EAM room. That

is where they had the card keypunch machines, sorters and collators.

To make a good impression, I also drew up flowcharts of the way the batch computer systems executed on a daily basis. I also helped out in the Staging Area. This is where these batch jobs were prepped for execution. I made my presence known throughout Data Processing. Eventually, everyone could see that I was eager and hungry. I had a good personality, so I got along with everyone. It was important to build solid professional relationships. I had to come off like I truly cared (which I did) and was not there to be a threat to anyone. After seven months I was promoted into the computer room. At this stage of my young career it was a major accomplishment to be promoted into that big glass room with the raised floor full of IBM mainframes and associated peripherals.

## Did I Miss Out on My Childhood?

People who know just how regimented I was at such a young age are constantly asking me: Don't you feel like you missed out on your childhood? Don't you feel like you were rushed through a very important part of your life?" Yes, you could say my youth was regimented, robotic even, and much too serious. Perhaps I did press the fast-forward button and rushed through my teenage years quicker than I should have. But I have no regrets because I accomplished ten times more in my teenage years than all of my five closest friends combined. For the record, I also had just as much fun, if not more so, than my peers.

Granted, my definition of fun differed greatly from theirs. They liked partying all the time. I, on the other hand, liked doing worthwhile things with my life. They only cared about temporary pleasures such as girls, drugs and alcohol. But I focused on making money, planning for the future, and if there was any time left over, then I'd chase a girl or two of my own. My circle of friends and I liked going out to the lake on the weekends, but it was a two-hour drive. Since I was the only car owner in the group and sober all the time, it was up to me to get us there.

Don't get me wrong, I wasn't always working. I dated—had girlfriends, went on vacations, and I enjoyed cruising in my beautiful, shiny car. I was the only one in the bunch who actually had something tangible to show for those teenage years besides great memories. How many teenagers can say they owned a brand new car and a nice home? Not only had I acquired these possessions as a teenager, but I also had a hefty savings account and a promising career. Unfortunately, my friends didn't accumulate anything until long after they had graduated from high school. Well, at least some of them tried to, anyway. Without having developed any sort of structure or discipline in their early years, they had a hard time surviving. That is the biggest difference between my lifestyle and the one they chose to live. They did the bare minimum every day while I never stopped excelling. I got out of bed with a purpose and they chose to lounge around until the afternoon.

## AGE NINETEEN: BECOMING A FIRST-TIME HOME -BUYER

True to form, when I turned eighteen, my dad collected one hundred dollars from me for rent. I respected that, and I was happy to oblige. In one way it felt good to contribute to the household; after all, my parents had sacrificed so much for my brother and me. They did everything in their power to give us the opportunity to make something with our lives.

I didn't like paying rent. It was like flushing money down the toilet. Although the rent was going to help support my family, it was still rent. It was still a four-letter word.

One of my major goals was to purchase a home before I turned twenty. Why was age twenty so important? I felt like it would even be more rewarding to accomplish this goal in my teens. Not too many teens can claim this type of accomplishment. Besides, I wanted to exit my teens with a major bang. That's what excited me—that's what turned me on.

I knew the time was near. I had been saving for five years now—yes, by this time I had made some major purchases. However, with each purchase I made sure it was part of my long-term plans. The grandest purchase of all was going to be that first home. It was a huge sacrifice and a burdensome debt to take on all alone at such a young age. This responsibility and sacrifice was like no other. From that time on, I was going to be on the hook for a mortgage and I wasn't even married. Even if I lost my job, I would still have to make that monthly payment. The bank wouldn't care whether or not I got laid off. They were not going to give me a reprieve. I was really nervous to pull the trigger because I knew my life would never be the same. I felt the heavy load of debt on my shoulders.

When you purchase that first home, the priority becomes that house. In other words, you have to budget around the household. You have to think long and hard before purchasing that expensive new sofa or that really fancy entertainment centre that will put you further into debt. The priority is making sure that your mortgage payment is paid in full and on time, and you always have enough money in savings to pay at least one year's worth of payments.

Although at this age I had the money for a good down payment, I wanted to have enough in the bank to make a year's worth of payments in case of an emergency. I also wanted to have a big enough down payment so the payments didn't strap me down every month.

Shortly after I turned nineteen, I purchased a townhouse in Westborough, California. It was approximately fifteen minutes south of San Francisco. It was an incredible yet scary process. The home was only a few years old. It had two bedrooms and two baths with a one car garage. It was located in the Silicon Valley between San Francisco and San Jose—it was a very good investment.

I only purchased a few things for the townhome initially. As mentioned above, furniture wasn't a priority—making sure I could always pay my monthly mortgage payment was much more important. Emergencies happen, and I was mentored by my neighbor to always be prepared for the worst. It's something you need to get comfortable with. I lived by a budget. Mortgage payments, utility bills, insurance payments, taxes, gas and food came first. I also wanted to keep saving, although the amount was going to be less. I still had to save. Savings was in my blood.

I remember purchasing an inexpensive bed at a department store and a couple of discounted bean bag chairs at Kmart. My parents gave me one of our older TVs and a table and chairs. I liked listening to the news when I was cooking or cleaning. That was pretty much it.

The first few months were pretty stressful, but then, after several mortgage payments, I felt comfortable being a homeowner. However, being comfortable didn't excite me. Please don't misunderstand me; I don't mean being comfortable relaxing in my home. I meant getting complacent. Being complacent was a lifestyle I wanted no part of. My neighbor Jim told me over and over again, "You're on this planet only once. Never be complacent—you never know when your number will be called and you're gone." It's a brutal way to state something, but oh so true!

After saving a few years, it was time to get a bigger home. Then I wanted a second home. I felt real estate was always a good investment.

# Ages Twenty to Twenty-nine

## LIVING LIKE TOMORROW WAS NEVER GOING TO COME

By this time in my life, I had accomplished some great goals, yet it wasn't enough for me. I was excelling in my career and my exercise regimen was getting more and more intense. Needless to say that my confidence level was sky-high. It wasn't enough—it was never enough—was my battle cry. I wanted to squeeze a lot more out of life. I kept thinking that at the rate I was going, I'd be an old man before I accomplished all of my major goals. There had to be another way to make things happen at a much quicker pace. I felt that I could conquer the world. I wanted to conquer it yesterday—but how? What would make me push harder, sleep less, be more creative, more resourceful and be resilient to negative emotions?

Eventually it came to me in the form of three simple words: *live with urgency*. For me this meant making every minute count—*not* hour. It dawned on me that the only way to make this happen was to train my mind to believe that I was going to have an expiration date sooner than later. Think about it, if people know they have half a century more to live, then what's the rush to accomplish anything? I picked my fortieth birthday as my do or die deadline.

You may feel inclined to ask, why is age forty a make or

break number for success? Forty is considered old by society's standards, such as getting into the military, starting a career, graduating from college, getting married, and starting a family. Now that is not to say you can't do these things at forty—many still do. Although certain things are much more difficult to start at forty, like becoming a profession athlete or perhaps starting out in law school—it's not impossible. Typically, by this age you've either made it in life or you haven't—for most. There are many who've beaten the odds—I actually know a few dozen.

To improve your odds for success, you need to *live with urgency.* Why not live life like your fortieth birthday is going to be your stamp of death? If you were thirty years old and you knew that death was coming for you in ten years instead of in another fifty, wouldn't you do everything to accomplish your goals as quickly as possible? Wouldn't you work hard and fast to leave behind a legacy for your loved ones? Wouldn't you stop procrastinating once and for all?

Wouldn't you live life with urgency every day? Of course you would. So, why not train your mind to believe that life ends at forty? Trick your mind into believing that you will die at forty; then you'll do everything possible (jump through hoops) to get things done yesterday, and not tomorrow or the next day.

## THE PROPOSAL THAT CHANGED MY LIFE

I went to one of the biggest car shows in California. It was held at the Oakland Coliseum in Oakland, California. This was the granddaddy of all car shows. Some of the most beautiful cars in the world were exhibited at this event. I was given free tickets, otherwise I wouldn't have gone—if you've seen one, well, you've pretty much seen them all.

It's there that I met an up-and-coming custom painter by the name of Mike Farley. He was standing near a custom-built motorcycle he had painted. It was awesome. His work stood out above the rest. He had that special touch I was seeking. I grabbed his card with the intention of getting back to him regarding a well-thought out proposal that could help him and benefit me at the same time. Custom painting was very expensive and of course I didn't want to deplete my savings paying for a custom paint job. You see, I had an idea that I believed would really turn heads.

A week went by, and I decided to visit Mr Farley at his paint shop. Once again, my chutzpa took over and led the way. I drove my car to his shop on a particularly sunny Saturday morning. The car was immaculate as always. You couldn't see a speck of dust anywhere, and the chrome was sparkling in the sun—you couldn't miss it. It was such a beautiful sight to behold.

## GRACED THE COVER OF *HOT ROD* MAGAZINE

My master plan was to have him custom-paint my car in a candy-apple maroon color with flames as well as a speed boat (a flat-bottom Sanger V-drive) that I was going to eventually purchase. Yes, that's right, a boat that I would *eventually* buy. My intention was for Mike to paint the car and boat the same colors so they would be a matching set. I've always been a stickler for wanting things that only an elite few could ever boast about having. I explained to Mike that I would help him prep (sand, tape, etc.) the car and boat and all he would have to do was paint. But that alone wasn't an attractive-enough proposition. That would have benefited me, but not him. To sweeten the pot for Mike, I promised to help him do prep work on other cars he was painting free of charge while my car and boat were in his shop.

Once the package deal was complete, I told him I would get him a ton of publicity by bringing my new works of art to all the big custom car shows, and market his talents for free. I would display a large poster advertising that the car and boat were painted by Mike Farley. But that was just the tip of the iceberg. I even went the extra mile and told Mike that I would find a way to get *Hot Rod* magazine to feature my car and boat. Amazingly, he agreed to all my terms. He must have seen the sincerity and determination in me—my chutzpa paid off big-time.

I worked at Mike's shop on weekends and evenings prepping my car and boat as well as others. In one year's time my car and boat were on the front cover of the July 1975 issue of *Hot Rod* magazine. It also won Best of Class in every car show I entered.

Now here's one of the greatest benefits of having a car and boat that graced the front cover of *Hot Rod* magazine when you are only twenty-one years old—hot chicks, and plenty of them. My methodical and hardworking teenage years paid off in spades, turning me into a highly coveted bachelor driving this car and boat to the lake every weekend.

## CLIMBED THE CORPORATE LADDER WITHOUT A FORMAL EDUCATION BUT WITH CHUTZPAH

At this time, I was in my fourth year at GTE Lenkurt. I had been promoted four times already. My life was consumed trying to make a mark in Information Technology (IT). The age of computing was just really getting started, with the big IBM mainframes. I'll never forget the first time an IBM mainframe computer and peripherals (tape drives, massive amounts of disk storage and a new high-speed printer) were purchased and set up in our newly built computer room with an elevated floor. I remember the flashing lights on the display panel. The lights were always flashing—except when there was a problem. When that happened, it was a catastrophe. It meant the systems were down, and there were a lot of people unable to access their big green monitors to input data.

Reflecting back, I believe that's one of the main reasons I was attracted to the world of computing in the first place. There was *never* a dull moment. Not only was technology critical to the company, it was constantly evolving. It seemed like almost every day there was some new hardware or software that needed to be evaluated. Also, the technology used in our existing infrastructure was always being upgraded. There were never enough hours in a day to keep up with it all—and certainly not in an eight-hour window of time. Actually, if you just worked eight hours, you would have never survived in the world of Information Technology. It was like no other industry for several reasons:

- The computers had to always be operational.
- Technology was constantly evolving, and our internal customers always wanted the latest and greatest—you constantly needed to stay abreast of new software and hardware that would benefit the business.
- Overly-demanding users. They always wanted more training on the latest and greatest technology to make them more efficient, therefore, more productive.

Trying to keep up with it was a monumental challenge. The long hours and dedication coupled with my tenacity led to many accomplishments that helped me get promoted frequently. I wanted to be promoted every year, but it was unrealistic of me to think it could happen. It doesn't mean I didn't keep trying. With each promotion came a bigger paycheck to support my family. I mean, who doesn't like more money, right?

The senior management came to know perfectly well who I was—the go-to guy. They knew that I would get the job done under any circumstances—regardless of how big or complex the challenge was.

## GETTING MYSELF INTO TOP PHYSICAL SHAPE

I was exercising seven days a week at a nearby gym. It opened at five and I was typically there around a little before then, in case the doors were opened a bit early. I was always eager to get my day started. There was no better feeling then waking up and getting that workout in. Once I was done with my exercise routine, the wheels in my brain would begin turning. It was one of the most awesome feelings in the world. I was always focused, and wanting to outdo my previous best. My toughest critic and worst enemy turned out to be myself. I would constantly play mind games to push myself harder. The mind games I resorted to were simple lines I repeated over and over again. For example:

- You're a wimp, push harder.
- Do you want to look like shit for the rest of your life?
- Is that all you can do?
- You're lazy—get going!

Working in Silicon Valley in the summertime definitely had its benefits—one of the biggest was the weather. At lunch time a group of us would go out for a run. Yep, I usually ended up getting in a double workout each day. It certainly recharged the batteries to help with the afternoon workload. You know how we all occasionally feel a bit sluggish in the afternoon. Consistently exercising was critical for maintaining the energy needed to operate at a high level. Feeling lazy or sluggish wasn't in my vocabulary. Consistent exercise was, and still is, a big success factor in my life.

## ADAPTING TO THE MARRIED LIFE

Tying the knot made my life a bit more complicated and challenging. Up until getting married, it had always been me, myself and I. Now there was someone else in the picture which added a new priority in my life. Now I had to factor the relationship with my wife into everything I did. At least I wanted to believe that. I thought it would be rather simple. That goes to show how naive I really was. For ten years before getting married, I had programmed my mind to believe that health and career were both the top priorities in my life and everything else was secondary. Actually, it was just career, because I considered health to be an extension of my professional life. Exercising regularly was the secret weapon I had that gave me the energy to be much more productive.

I mistakenly thought I could de-program myself easily to incorporate a relationship. In other words, instead of having two priorities, from that point on, I would have three. It didn't take me long at all to find out that it wasn't that easy. After years of programming myself to be robotic with my priorities of career and health, with everything else being secondary, it was not a switch I could make in one fluid move.

Personal relationships had always come second. This was

undoubtedly one of the highest-costing mistakes I'd ever made. Although I said all the right things to my wife as far as priorities go, my routine didn't change a bit. It was always all about me, and my wife got easily lost in the background.

Unfortunately, I didn't put the same emphasis on my personal relationships as I did on my professional ones. In other words, my wife took a backseat to my career and that gym. I had trained my mind to follow a set routine around the clock, come what may. I was programmed—just like a machine. Subconsciously, I didn't want to change, even though I said I would, dozens of times. So for sixteen years my wife tolerated *my* flawed priorities and *my* inflated ego. I couldn't change it if my life depended on it. I didn't know how to, at the time.

My wife was a good woman. She loved me very much. She understood me and was proud of what I had accomplished, but my invincible mindset was as strong as ever—actually, it became stronger with each new accomplishment. I was unstoppable. I couldn't help myself. I loved the thrill of excelling in my career. It was the biggest turn-on for me, when that should have been my family life.

# Ages Thirty to Thirty-nine

## OPTIMIZING MY SLEEPING PATTERNS

I was already sleeping fewer hours than most (by choice). I was already driven and efficient from being so disciplined all those years, however, I just needed more hours each day to accomplish more. The clock was ticking, and I wanted to solidify my legacy. Was that egotistical on my part? Sure it was! You get but one life to live—why not leave a legacy?

In my mind, there was only one thing left to do, and that was to drastically reduce the time I spent sleeping. My end goal was to get it down to four hours consistently each day. This was no easy feat. I was already averaging between five to six hours of sleep a night. My training began by telling myself repeatedly that oversleeping was a waste of time. Even lounging in bed for ten to twenty minutes can be a huge time-waster. It's the equivalent of extrapolating twenty minutes a day throughout the year. Eventually, it all adds up.

Since I wanted to accomplish more, I started experimenting with reducing the amount of sleep. To me, sleep was a waste of time, but a necessity to re-charge your batteries. However, I wanted just the bare minimum to still thrive and not compromise on my health. Lucky for me, over time I had built up a strong constitution, and all the years of living a healthy lifestyle helped me to function well with reduced sleep.

I tackled this *enormous* challenge by reducing the amount of time I slept by half an hour every two weeks. I also would pace myself during the day so that I did brain-intensive activities when I was most alert. I talked to myself (repeating relevant lines), affirming that I didn't need much sleep. It wasn't easy, but in time I was able to get my body used to functioning on four hours of sleep a night. I did this thirty years ago! Now here comes my legal disclaimer: *I am not a doctor, and I am offering my own life experience only as information for you.*

I fully realize that in these days of intense demand on time, many people are trying to find more hours in the day. I don't recommend my four-hour craziness to anyone; however, if you're someone who is sleeping between –eight-ten hours a night, you may want to consider reducing it to –seven-eight hours—if you are in good health and have consulted with your primary care physician.

## THE LIFE OF A MULTI-PUBLISHED AUTHOR AND INTERNATIONAL MOTIVATIONAL SPEAKER

I was upbeat, positive and always looking forward, but I trained my mind that negative things would happen when I least expected it. By no means was I a negative person. I just wanted to be prepared for the unexpected. The one thing you can count on in this life is that negative things *will* happen, that are out of your control. Sometimes medical emergencies can't be helped, regardless of how healthy you are. As for employment, most of us will be laid off at least once in our lives. The trick is to be prepared to weather the storm. Most individuals are blindsided by life's unexpected curveballs, and the results are disastrous. They lose everything: their home, car, medical coverage, and other necessities. Please don't let this happen to you.

One area in which you can be thoroughly prepared is your career. Ideally, you should get yourself into a position where you have multiple streams of income. In time, and depending on how the economy fluctuates, the one or two sources that your family counts on could eventually dry up.

I've always been a firm believer that you shouldn't put all your eggs in one basket. Although I was already an executive at a multi-billion dollar Fortune 500 company, I knew that the higher you climbed the ladder, the more brutal the politics was. I needed insurance—*never* think that your career is secure. It *never* will be. This is why precisely you should always strategize for alternative sources of income.

At this stage of my life I had established some extremely aggressive goals which were:

- Write an IT management book
- Get that IT book published
- Publish a series of IT management books
- Publish a series of self-discipline related books
- Become a motivational speaker
- Start an IT consulting business
- Start a life coaching business

My overall objective was to have my name synonymous with IT management and self-discipline. This way I could always get IT consulting work or have a career in the already saturated self-help industry. To do that, I needed tons of credibility. I needed to set myself apart from the rest. I needed to build a portfolio that wasn't second to none. It was time to write and do it non-stop.

I wrote around the clock. My first IT book was published

by Prentice Hall (PTR) in 1994. It was titled, *Rightsizing the New Enterprise: The Proof, Not the Hype.* The book quickly became a bestseller with PTR. I was ecstatic, but the excitement wore off quickly. It was just another accomplished goal.

One morning while working in my office the president of PTR called to congratulate me, and in the same sentence, asked if I could write a sequel as quickly as possible. Little did he know that I was already working on the sequel. It was all part of my game plan. Again, I was writing around the clock every chance I got. My laptop went with me everywhere. My second book was titled *Managing the New Enterprise.* The third book in line was titled *Networking the New Enterprise* and the fourth, *Building the New Enterprise.*

After having published four books with PTR, I wanted to do something out-of-the-box. I wanted to have my own series of IT management books with PTR. In other words, publish dozens of books under the Harris Kern/PTR label.

Because the sales of my first four books were good, I requested a meeting with Greg Doench, a senior executive with Prentice Hall in charge of sales for all technology books. My idea was to establish a series of IT management "howto" books. The meeting went well and shortly thereafter, we launched Harris Kern's Enterprise Computing Institute. I solicited other professionals to be co-authors to grow my new series. I was constantly seeking new themes/titles/potential writers to join my new little publishing company. This took a lot of cycles, but was well worth it in the end. My portfolio and credibility in the IT industry was growing quickly.

So there I was, promoting my books all over the world and making tens of thousands of dollars in royalty income alone. In the interim, I developed into a dynamic speaker, and my books were my calling card.

By my calculations, I traveled over four million miles—probably 80 per cent of the time. The only upside about flying was that it gave me the opportunity to write more books. The traveling was all done while working at my full-time corporate job at Sun Microsystems in Palo Alto, CA. I was managing an organization of over 350 people. I must have consistently worked seventy hours every single week.

There were many sacrifices I was forced to make during this period. Spending quality time with my daughter was, by far, the worst one. I wasn't around enough to watch her grow up. It was a selfish decision. However, the one bright spot that stands out in my mind now is the time I did spend with her.

## LAUNCHING A SUCCESSFUL BUSINESS WHILE WORKING FULL-TIME AS A CORPORATE EXECUTIVE

I was a successful vice president at a Fortune 500 company, making a six-figure income. There was nothing getting in the way of me buying whatever I wanted. The problem was, I wanted to accomplish more out of my professional life. After giving it some thought, I realized that I wanted to start my own business and be my own boss. I was always like a sugar-craving kid with the key to a candy store and having free access anytime he wanted. There was no satisfying my hunger. I wanted more.

At this stage of my life I had a solid understanding of my strengths and weaknesses. I knew that to be successful in any small business, you needed to offer exceptional services and/or products. The first order of business was to find an exceptional salesman who had the gift of the gab. I needed someone who could sell practically anything under the sun. Fortunately, I didn't have to look far. He was actually someone who I had mentored before. He had drive, intelligence, and possessed the gift of the gab. He also happened to be charismatic. But more importantly, he also wanted to make something happen in his professional life. So, together, he and I decided to start an IT consulting services company.

My strategy was to leverage the series of books as my calling card to open doors to companies for the purpose of selling them my IT management services. Instead of giving potential customers T-shirts or coffee mugs, I would give them a copy of one of my books. It was a solid sales and marketing strategy that proved to be a winning formula. The books opened doors for our new consulting company. We were quickly earning money and became successful after the first full year of business.

# Ages Forty to Sixty

## SURVIVING A BRUTAL DIVORCE

You've probably heard dozens of horror stories about divorces that were downright nasty. Well, mine was definitely in that category. I wouldn't be surprised if it was rated among the top ten worst of all time. The worst part of the breakup was that my son disowned me, although I am hopeful that someday he will realize how much I have always loved him. Our estrangement tore me apart, and till this day, it still does. Actually, this was the most difficult section of the book for me to write. I still get all choked up just thinking about it. That will never change, because I miss him dearly.

The problems at home escalated during my days of flying all over the world speaking and consulting. I was traveling 80 per cent of the time and living the high life. I was treated like royalty everywhere I travelled. All the pampering and special attention finally got to me, and I went overboard with all the glitz and glamour. I ended up having several affairs which further destroyed an already flawed marriage.

As a result of my philandering ways, I lost more than half of my wealth. Due to the guilt eating away at me, I gave my ex-wife our $10,00,000 plus home, along with the furniture and family luxury car. I wanted to start a new life with a clean slate. At the age of forty, I started all over again. Because I was so disciplined and lived life with urgency, it didn't take me long to rebuild my wealth, and that was while paying a hefty amount for child support and alimony.

After the divorce, I focused all of my energy into rebuilding my empire. I wanted to own a beautiful home again. I had never been able to stomach living in an apartment, and I wasn't about to start at this stage of my life.

## MENTORED HUNDREDS OF PEOPLE TO BE MORE EFFICIENT

There's no greater feeling than helping someone become more productive. I decided to become a life coach and an organization performance mentor because I felt it was time to give back. My neighbor had taken valuable time out of his busy life to help me—now it was my turn to help others.

My approach has been thoroughly tested on hundreds of people who sorely needed guidance. I personally interact with every individual (seven days a week) via telephone, Skype, text and email. I am there alongside them through their trials, tribulations, and triumphs—attached to their hip (figuratively speaking) every step of the way! I tell them that when it comes to developing their self-discipline skills, there are no 9-5 Monday-Friday boundaries. It just doesn't work that way. If you have poor time management in your professional world, it carries over into your personal space. It takes a full-time commitment to become disciplined.

One of the things my clients appreciate about me is that I do not believe in failure. End of story. If they fail, then that makes me a failure as a mentor. The word *failure* doesn't exist in my vocabulary. I am extremely passionate when it comes to helping people succeed; there is nothing more rewarding than to watch them bloom before my eyes. Basically, my mentorship program is divided into two phases:

## Phase One: Assessment, Strategy and Roadmap

In order to predetermine a potential client's needs, I utilize a comprehensive questionnaire. I ask approximately one hundred questions. The assessment enables me to understand an individual's strengths, weaknesses, goals, career-related aspirations, relationship, leadership skills, financial situation, surroundings, hobbies, phobias, etc. I put myself in their shoes to understand and absorb their strengths and weaknesses. I will then give them a preliminary synopsis, which summarizes/prioritizes their challenges and explains the strategy involved to achieve results. I will also have a heart-to-heart discussion with them to make sure they're on-board for the journey.

Once the evaluation is complete and I have absorbed their issues, I will then develop a strategy and roadmap, which includes:

- Their initial goals from the evaluation process and any new ones if applicable.
- A synopsis of their life before the mentoring begins.
- A strategy to develop their self-discipline skills.
- An Action Plan with milestones and safeguards to ensure success.
- A new daily and weekend routine to establish structure in their life.

## Phase Two: Mentoring

The second phase is on-going mentoring, which includes monitoring and administration. I am involved with e-mail, text, Skype and phone calls daily (as many as required). I will monitor and track progress. I am diligent in holding everyone accountable to their target dates, ensuring consistency and successful completion of milestones.

All of my clients can see a difference in the direction of their lives and finally have confidence and hope that they will be able to achieve any goal once they have been able to put structure in their daily living through my guidance.

## SOLIDIFYING YOUR LEGACY

There isn't a greater feeling than knowing when I leave this planet that my children, friends, colleagues and people who I've helped over the years will have more than just pictures and memories left over. Sure, there will be the material possessions left for my loved ones. People will also remember me as being synonymous with self-discipline and the IT industry. The books will probably still be on Amazon for decades to come. However, for me personally helping others overcome their challenges has been an *extraordinary* high. I am hoping that those individuals will continue to thrive, and be a bit of my eternal fire for success.

My existence is to impact as many people who reach out to me for help as possible. My legacy is that my teachings will help them succeed long past I have departed. What about you? Will you die with just pictures and memories or do you want to leave behind a legacy to impact as many people as possible—especially your kids? What do you really want to have accomplished when you exit this world? What does life mean to you? Remember, life is only temporary, but your legacy could last forever.

I believe that our society has it wrong when they pontificate to us as youngsters to prepare for our retirement. Retirement is an ugly word in my book. Retirement has an expiration date. In other words, you hit a certain age and then you stop being productive—you just kick back and go fishing or playing golf every day. Whoopee, that just doesn't turn me on. God willing, if your mind is still intact in your forties, fifties, sixties, seventies and beyond that, why not make the most of it and help as many people as possible? Forget the word retirement and live the word legacy!

# My Special Relationship with God Now, My Number One Priority

My mom was very religious and practiced our Jewish faith daily. My dad could care less about religion. They were complete opposites. Mother would go to the temple at least once a week and my brother and I reluctantly accompanied her. I stopped going after my Bar mitzvah (thirteenth birthday). School, work, chores and friends kept me busy; I thought the excuses for not going were compelling enough.

My Bar mitzvah netted me approximately one thousand dollars (I don't recall the exact amount). However, it was a lot of money for a thirteen-year old in 1967. I quickly put the funds into the bank, which was a major adrenalin rush for me. The feeling of having money was awesome. I wanted more, a great deal more and in a hurry—I became money hungry. Money was real, that was tangible, and God at that time wasn't for me. I even stopped praying because I was always strategizing on how to make my next dollar. In retrospect; turning my back on God was the worst mistake of my life, and I've made plenty—just like everyone else.

I thought being disciplined and successful would fulfill every aspect of my life. Boy, was I wrong! I didn't know how warped my thinking was regarding spiritual matters until I reached my fifties. I had it all: money, credibility in my IT career and the self-help industry, multiple published books, decent looks, a nice physique, several homes, a beautiful wife, family, etc. I should have been elated with what I accumulated, but for some inexplicable reason I wasn't. In my mind, I was on top of the world, but in reality I was standing barefoot on top of an anthill. Sure, I was still a caring individual to some, but *not* all. Along my road to success, I hurt a lot of people and they were mostly all women. I loved women and I said what they wanted to hear just to get them in the sack. As much as it pains me to admit it, I cheated on my first wife. Then I hurt my second wife by putting my career first and not my family.

I was also an egotistical pig, and down deep inside I knew it. In my own mind, I was a big shot and untouchable. But the truth is, my self-perception was so distorted back then. I wasn't really who I thought I was. Please don't think this is just another born-again Christian testimonial. Actually, I wasn't even raised as a Christian. I was raised a Jew. So, I certainly couldn't fit into that profile. The first fifty years of my existence was all about Harris Kern. It's always been about me. Now, at the age of sixty, it's all about Jesus Christ and my family.

If you're lucky enough to live a half century (like me), you *realize* that every day from here forward is truly a blessing. Every day is a gift and every day of existence is because of a higher power. When I entered my fifties, I looked back to inventory the damage I had caused—it wasn't a pretty scene. In fact, it was downright *ugly*. I knew, based on my past behavior I wasn't going to be traveling north to the place where we all want to go after death. I was heading in the complete opposite direction.

## Forgiveness

The time had come to make amends and seek forgiveness from many people; and it started with my first wife. Mind you, I hadn't spoken to her in nearly twenty years when I decided to call her out of the blue. I wanted to offer my apologies—even if she hung up the phone on me. I had to try and ask her for forgiveness. It was strange to ask someone I hurt so badly for forgiveness, but it felt like a thousand pounds just came off my chest. I had a long list of people to contact. I continued the process throughout the next few days. Everyone accepted my apologies and I was grateful to God for that.

My life changed for the better when I was introduced to the good Lord Jesus Christ in the winter of 2013. I will never forget that Monday morning when I was on a business trip in Atlanta. What was supposed to be a one-time excursion eventually became a weekly commute from Dallas. On my first trip to visit my client, I was taking the shuttle van from the hotel to the office. The shuttle driver's name was Donald Stewart—an angel sent from God. For the first few weeks I had no idea that he was a priest—driving the shuttle van was his side job.

On my third or fourth week to Atlanta, I was having a bad week dealing with personal issues with my wife in Dallas—Donald could see it written all over my face. I confessed to him that I had some issues at home to deal with, and they were really affecting my ability to concentrate at work, at the gym, and everywhere I went. Commuting back and forth, I would sit in the front seat of the van next to Donald, because I never liked getting in the back seat. On this particular morning he asked me for my pinky. Even though I thought it was a strange request, I complied. He then said a heart-felt prayer. Unfortunately, I don't remember the exact words, but I do recall him thanking the Lord Jesus for that wonderful morning. Donald then asked me if I had read the Bible. I told him that it was too difficult for me to comprehend—every time I tried I was totally lost after a few paragraphs.

The next morning he brought me a book titled *Jesus Calling*, written by Sarah Young. The book was filled with devotions, one for every day of the year. He instructed me to never read ahead. "You can only read the current day's devotion, and as much as you want to read from previous days," he said to me. It was a great feeling to wake up every morning and read my daily devotion while drinking a cup of coffee. It's been several years, and I still read it daily. That book, Donald and my Lord Jesus Christ saved my life. I haven't been the same ever since.

Donald also called, texted or emailed me throughout the day. Without a doubt Jesus sent Donald to save my soul. I am finally at peace with myself—to an extent. Yes, I have put Jesus in the front and center in my life, but that's not enough. I have repented my sins, but I never want to forget my wrongdoings. I have moved forward, but I still want to feel the pain that I have caused others. This will *not* change for me. I will punish myself for the sins I have committed for the rest of my life. This may sound contradictory to what I've written in my self-help books and what others have said about not dwelling in the past. But it's important for me as a human being to grow spiritually by never, even for one moment, forgetting my past. I don't dwell on it, but I keep it front and center just like God.

## I am Now at Ease Until He Calls

It's all about you and your relationship with God—*not how many toys you have and still want*. Please don't make the same mistake I did. I focused on two priorities (career and health) and of course relationships with women. There wasn't time left over for God. I wanted more toys and more play time. That was a great feeling, a continuous high—right? Who wouldn't be happy with more toys and women...oh, was I stupid! Thank God I was able to see through my egotistical needs and the importance of faith in my life.

With God, everything is possible. Make him the first and foremost priority in your life. It will change the way you think about everything. You will have purpose every day. I will give my time (which is the most valuable asset I have) to help others for the rest of my life as Donald helped me so frequently. I will spread God's goodness as far as I humanly can.

I was always afraid that putting God first would slow me down from accomplishing goals at lightning speed with a laser-like focus, but the complete opposite has happened. I still live life with urgency, but also realize that I am on borrowed time. Every day is a blessing, so I will continue to make use of every minute, but I will also put God first to make my existence on this planet worthwhile. Jesus, thank you for blessing me with today.

# Appendix

As noted in the introduction, there are Existers and there are people who wake up with a purpose every day and make something happen. Below are some of the quotes I hear from Existers:

*I live life one day at a time*

If you sincerely want to get ahead and make something of your life, you need a well- documented plan and a trained mind to consistently hold yourself accountable to execute. Nobody has ever become successful by doing as the title above implies. Success (however you define it) cannot be achieved by living life by the seat of your pants. Success is measured by lifelong accomplishments. With accomplishments come happiness, confidence and purpose. This phrase is meant for someone recovering from a major illness or getting over a traumatic experience.

*It can wait until tomorrow*

I hate it when people tell me tomorrow is another day—relax! With that kind of attitude, you might as well wait until next week/month. What's the difference? For me, every minute of every day is precious, and once wasted will *never* come back. Don't keep pushing things off until the next day—you will never get ahead. As a matter of fact, you will only get further and further behind. Instill a sense of urgency to be productive every day of the year. With a laidback attitude, accomplishments will be few and far between.

*I need at least eight hours of sleep a night*

You complain there's never enough time in a day to get everything you need done, but on the other hand, you sleep eight, nine or even ten hours every night and probably more on the weekend. And if you add up the time you lounge in bed every morning after the alarm goes off...no wonder you don't have enough time in the day. As highlighted throughout the book, you have no choice but to be more efficient and productive at an accelerated pace. Who has the luxury of sleeping eight-ten hours a day anymore? Even if you do have the time, I think your most valuable resource could be better utilized. So-called sleep experts have said you need at least eight hours for as far back as I can remember. Who wouldn't want to get eight hours consistently?

From the hundreds of life coaching evaluations I've facilitated, it is apparent that people waste far too much time sleeping and lounging around in bed far too long. There's no reason why they couldn't cut back on their sleep or lounging time by thirty-sixty minutes. As long as you take care of your health (eating right and exercise consistently), go for it.

I've been living on four hours' sleep for the past thirty years. Please don't emulate me, however there's no reason why you can't experiment and cut your sleep time a bit to see if that works for you. Just think about all the goals you could be working on with that extra seven hours a week.

*Here comes my legal disclaimer:*

I am not a doctor. I am merely offering my own life experience as information for you. I do NOT recommend you to sleep only four hours a day.

*What are your New Year's resolutions?*

Why do people waste their time making up New Year's resolutions year after year? Have you ever tried to complete a major goal at work without a strategy and formal plan? Then how can you make up a goal at the spur of the moment and expect to actually accomplish it without a well thought out plan, which includes key milestones? And, if you need to start a goal based on a special day, then chances are you will not be successful in your endeavor. Don't establish New Year's resolutions—it's a total waste of time.

*I'm too tired to exercise*

Who isn't too tired to exercise? There are dozens of excuses that anyone can think of on any given day for not exercising. The number one reason to do it consistently is to keep yourself healthy. I typically start my exercise routine anywhere from 3:00 to 4:00 a.m. *every* morning. It's a great way to start the day, and it sets the tempo. By 5:00 a.m. the wheels are spinning at full speed. I don't need a cup of coffee to wake me up. There are better and healthier ways to get yourself going each morning. Make it a point to find what works for you. You will not believe the benefits until you apply them for yourself.

Am I ever tired and don't feel like exercising? Heck, probably four days of the week I am tired and don't feel like exercising—who isn't tired at that time of the morning? However, I've trained my mind to not give in to the temptation of staying in bed, and pretty much force myself to get up and make it happen by not allowing myself to sleep anymore. Even if I wanted to sleep more or lounge in bed, my mind wouldn't let me do it. Train your mind to exercise daily—it's the only solution.

*I don't feel good*

I can think of at least a few dozen times in a year that I don't feel very well (upset stomach, headache, cold, general aches and pains), but it doesn't mean that everyone has to know about it or that I'm going to sit there doing nothing, and feel sorry for myself. Just the opposite should happen. If you train your mind, it will force you to get off your butt and make something happen. It will not allow you to dwell on pain (emotional or physical); it will help you work right through it.

In general, people whine too much. Society has turned most of us into wimps. You always hear people complaining about all their aches and pains. They want you to feel sorry for them. I guess that old saying "misery loves company" holds true. I am sixty years old and have all kinds of minor aches and pains from working out every day of the year, but that's between me, myself and I. My mind is so well trained that it just keeps telling me that I cannot be broken, over and over again, and then go attack the day.

*It's not whether you win or lose, it's how you play the game*

It's always about winning, and it should always be about winning! No one should ever feel good about losing! Yes, we should play by the rules and apply our values at all times while doing our very best to win. All I'm saying is that you should always play to win. Winning can be just as habit-forming as losing. They are both very addictive, so take your pick. It is

better to train your mind in a positive way by telling yourself
that you will win and take every step to reach that goal. If
you simply follow the words of the above phrase throughout
life then you may never really give it your best effort to reach
your goals, minor and major. If you have honestly given your
best and lose at something, then you can say you really did
play to win, and next time you will try harder, and yes, you
played the game as best as you could.

*I'm so stressed out—I need a vacation*

The word "stress" is over-utilized in our society. Some is
definitely warranted due to pressures at home (dealing with
drama) or at the office (management deadlines or politics).
Unfortunately, most stress is self-induced. The majority of
people are stressed because they have failed to manage their
time well. When we severely procrastinate and wait until the
last minute to finish something, then of course we're stressed.
But whose fault is that? We all have problems (personal,
health, financial, etc.), and there are some days when those
problems are unbearable. Once your mind is trained and you
live life like you are dying, you will effectively and efficiently
manage your life, and the 'S' word will be minimally used in
your vocabulary.

*Be happy with what you have*

You should give thanks for what you have every day, but *never*
be satisfied with what you have accomplished to date. Always
strive for more—once your mind has been trained, you will
constantly strive for perfection. You will have no choice—
so don't bother fighting it. I get a major rush every time I
accomplish something, so why would I ever want that feeling
to stop? You can have anything you want, whether they are

material things or not. If you stay focused and work hard enough you will be much happier with even the tiniest goals, because of the string of milestones you accomplished every day to attain that goal.

*Stop and smell the roses*

In this day and age when you're asked to do more with less time, there is less time to stop and smell the roses. Because I work so hard, it appears that I don't take time to do this, but that couldn't be further from the truth. My motivation for working hard is to accomplish more and to spend ample time having fun with my family. If you remain structured and live life with urgency, there is ample time for work and play. When you remain structured (abiding by your priorities, being organized, following a to-do list and adhering to an efficient routine), you will be more productive and manage your life (career, health and relationships) much more efficiently. By ensuring that all personal and professional activities are included on your daily to-do list, you will maintain balance. To ensure there's ample time for play, include fun activities on your to-do list. If it's out of sight, then it will rarely happen.

*Failure is ok as long as you keep trying*

Don't ever tell yourself that failure is ok. It's not ok! If you're easy on yourself (i.e., by repeatedly telling yourself it's ok to fail, just keep trying again) then chances are you run the risk of always failing. Be afraid to death of failure. Tell yourself repeatedly that it's the worst thing that could possibly happen. Scare yourself into thinking that if you fail once you may set yourself up for an endless string of upsets in the future. Do or say whatever you want to yourself to make sure you don't fail. Do whatever it takes to ensure success!

*Dieting*

Don't! Just manage your caloric intake. Diets don't work for a prolonged period of time. They're only temporary solutions to a lifelong problem. The solution is making health (consistently exercising and eating right) a priority in your life. Once maintaining good health is a priority, manage your eating habits appropriately. Keep it simple. Watch your daily caloric and carbohydrate intake. If you eat too much one day, then cut back considerably for the next few days. Everyone loves good food and enjoys cheating occasionally, so do I, but if I cheat one day, I will cut back considerably the next few days. Never diet—always manage.

*Retirement*

Why? To play golf every day, go fishing every day, or get up and do nothing. Wow, how exciting! I don't like the word retirement because it carries such a negative message. I know it may sound harsh, but in my opinion retirement or letting your mind go dormant is such a waste. I can see taking it easy a bit when you start getting up there in age, but don't stop production altogether. Hey, you can still play golf a few days a week, but don't sit around and turn that wonderful mind of yours completely off. There's still so much for you to accomplish.

*My intentions were there*

"Begin somewhere.
You cannot build a reputation on
what you intend to do."

**Liz Smith**

Intentions don't mean anything. Anyone can have as many intentions as they can dream up, but where the rubber meets the road is when you follow through with each and every commitment. Failure to follow through on just one commitment is wrong and you will quickly lose respect from your friends and colleagues. You will be labeled as just a talker. It's sad to say, but there are more talkers than doers. Don't be a 'yes' person. If you can't manage your life effectively, how do you expect to find the resources to help others?

*Pinning false hopes on the new year*

Good wishes around the holidays won't change a thing. Some of my favorites are: "I hope you have a good New Year and I hope this New Year brings you good health, happiness and success." Folks, you need to get a grip here. Mere words alone will not give you a better life. It's not the well-wishers I'm aggravated with, it's those who really think the calendar is going to change their lives! And hoping and praying won't do it either.

Do you honestly think because it's 1 January that you will have a chance for a fresh start in life? Please tell me what the difference between 31 December and 1 January is. It's a day—that's it. Get disciplined and live your precious life with urgency to be productive. It takes hard work to change your life around, not some silly date on the calendar.

*Big is beautiful*

If you're overweight. please don't con yourself into believing that being fat is beautiful. Let's stop playing make believe because being overweight is not beautiful, and more importantly it's extremely unhealthy. If you keep telling yourself that it's beautiful, you'll never lose the weight. Look in the mirror and be honest with yourself. Be dissatisfied—be disgusted. If you are unhappy with how you look and your health is being compromised then it's time to start doing something about it. Do yourself a favor and seek help through a counselor, support group or exercise program. You owe it to yourself to treat your body with respect and take care of it. People care about you and your health.

*Living in the dreams of possibility and hope—not in the reality of today*

The word hope is only reserved for those times when things are totally out of your control (i.e., someone is ill or suffering a trauma, etc.). Don't spend your entire life hoping things are going to happen for you automatically. You will fail miserably and many people could be negatively impacted, especially your family. If you're unproductive, you have no choice but to make something happen now. It won't miraculously occur on its own.

You're in control of your life. Be disciplined by developing your self-discipline skills (read my book titled *Going from Undisciplined to Self-mastery*) and live life by being efficient, so you're consistently productive and accomplishing your goals.

## LINES FOR PEOPLE WHO LIVE

*Whatever it takes*

> "Hell, there are no rules here—we're trying to accomplish something."

### Thomas A. Edison

Simply put, you need to do whatever it takes to complete a goal or project on schedule. Just completing a goal is not enough, do whatever it takes to complete a goal by its scheduled due date. When trying to accomplish your goals, following what Thomas Edison said above is best. "There are no rules here." Do whatever it takes to complete a goal. I probably use this quote more than any other quote because I truly believe that's what made me successful. I was always doing whatever it took to accomplish another goal.

*Just do it*

If you think you can do it then make it happen, but there has to be commitment, passion and focus behind each and every goal. Make sure you've planned your new goal out thoroughly, and it needs to be on your radar. In other words, there needs to be milestones associated with each goal that is on your to-do list every day. That to-do list should be next to you throughout the day. No excuses for not following a to-do list. You can't be successful without that list!

*Nothing worthwhile comes easy—you need to earn it*

No pain, no gain. To live a happy, balanced and extremely productive life means being disciplined and living life with urgency. It will not be easy, especially in the first year or so, when you're trying to train your mind to hold yourself accountable.

Mastering your life is hard work. This is reality, and I don't want to sugarcoat the effort. But to me (and I hope for most of you reading this) what's a little pain and hard work for something this worthwhile?

It will force you to put structure into your life. It means being on a strict routine every day of the week, and yes, that includes weekends. It means being organized and focusing on your daily to-do list. You're now on the clock, where every minute has a price tag. You're suddenly managing your life as if it were a business. Sure it's hard work, but nothing in your lifetime will be this rewarding. It will change your life forever, and for the better!

*Take small steps*

Don't just set goals first. Establish your priorities. I recommend *health*, *career* and *relationships* as the three most important areas to focus on. Once you've established priorities, set realistic goals. Be conservative. You need to get used to successes consistently, not failures. After setting realistic goals, establish daily milestones for each goal. One of the biggest mistakes people make is taking their goals on without establishing milestones. You should focus on these milestones (small steps) to ensure successful goal completion.

For each priority, establish several goals, but do not set goals that are unrealistic. Let's say that one of your goals under the priority of health is to lose fifty pounds. Once you establish goals, set daily milestones and focus on those small steps. If you're constantly thinking about that big goal, you will be overwhelmed, and potentially fail. Accomplishing those small steps will eventually add up to big accomplishments. Your milestones could be:

- Do some form of exercise daily.
- Eat no carbohydrates six days a week.
- Reduce caloric intake by 25 per cent from Monday to Friday.
- Reduce caloric intake on Saturday and Sunday by 10 per cent.

The hierarchy for successful goal management would look like:

1. Priorities
2. Goals
3. Milestones

*Winning is everything*

Winning is everything, and the sooner you get used to winning on a regular basis, the more success you will enjoy. The more wins you get, the more you want—it becomes addictive. This goes for your personal life (i.e., your personal best time in that last 10K race) as well as your professional life (i.e., that promotion you've been seeking).

*Training your mind*

To be successful in life, your mind has to be the pilot. It has all the power and controls. It will take you anywhere and everywhere, and if trained properly, it will hold you accountable and put your body in autopilot to help you take on your daily battles. It will never get tired or falter. Training your mind is the key to successful goal management and living your life with a sense of urgency.

*Time is money*

You need to equate every minute to money. The same way you would budget your finances to make every rupee count; every minute of your life needs to be managed properly and efficiently. Time is the most valuable resource you have—don't squander it!

*Success is not about money*

Success is all about accomplishments and being able to take your mind and body to new heights. With accomplishments there are rewards. There is no greater feeling in the world than completing another one of your goals ahead of schedule. On many instances, a by-product of some of these accomplishments is monetary, but that comes with the territory. Accomplishments last an eternity, money comes and goes.

*Life is all about leaving behind a legacy*

Is there anything else? We will all die—I'm keeping it simple. Heck, I can relate to that line. Do you want to just leave behind pictures on the mantle and nice memories or do you want to leave behind a legacy? I chose the latter. I wanted my disciplined mannerisms (especially to live life with a sense of urgency) to be emulated by my children so they won't waste precious resources (time and energy) to make the most of their future.

It worked with the proof, not the hype. I mentored them on how to be disciplined, making sure they understood that being disciplined will allow them to achieve just about anything. As they witnessed me consistently accomplish it, it rubbed off on them—in other words, seeing, truly, is believing.

*Don't be complacent—always strategize—strive for perfection*

There's always a more efficient way to get things done. Think out of the box at all times. Keep the wheels spinning at a high RPM and continuously strategize:

- How can I change my routine to become more efficient?
- How can I make my exercise routine more beneficial

and also keep it exciting?

- How can I expand my business?
- How can I complete my goals at an accelerated pace?
- How can I utilize my resources more efficiently?
- What can I do to help my daughter become more successful?

The bottomline is that becoming the best you can be is not rocket science. There's always a better method—never stop strategizing.

*Tell it like it is—always*

I have several life coaching clients who can't stand to be around negativity, but who would. Heck, I don't like it either. They get so choked up and actually start crying during our discussions. They come to me for motivation and I oblige, but this is a temporary fix. There is plenty of negativity everywhere. The sooner you train your mind to take that negative energy and turn it into a positive force, the more productive you will be. Train your mind to stay on track regardless of the situation.

## MY FAVORITE LINES

*I cannot be broken*

On those days when I hurt, or am tired, both my body and mind are at odds. My body is telling me to rest and my mind is telling me to keep going. My mind always wins. We've all been there on those days when we needed that little extra push. I've trained my mind by repeatedly telling myself that I cannot be broken. My mind takes over and motivates me to forget about any potential pains I may have on any given day.

*I'll sleep plenty when I die*

When my friends or family tell me to rest, they know the line that's coming right back at them. Think about it for a minute—it's true isn't it? It's one of my favorite and most frequently used lines.

*It's me against me—always*

I don't look up to anyone except God. I am not awed by great athletes or movie stars. I look in the mirror and see me, myself and I. What I see, I never like—I want to be better in everything I do. I am never satisfied, and I want to accomplish more before I die. I am my biggest enemy. Below is one of my favorite quotes:

THE GUY IN THE GLASS

*When you get what you want in your struggle for self*
*And the world makes you king for a day,*
*Then go to the mirror and look at yourself,*
*And see what the guy has to say.*

For it isn't your Father, or Mother, or Wife,

Who judgment upon you must pass.
The feller whose verdict counts most in your life
Is the guy staring back from the glass.

He's the feller to please, never mind all the rest,
For he's with you clear up to the end,
And you've passed your most dangerous, difficult test
If the guy in the glass is your friend.

You may be like Jack Horner and "chisel" a plum,
And you think you're a wonderful guy,

But the man in the glass says you're only a bum
If you can't look him straight in the eye.

You can fool the whole world down the pathway of years,
And get pats on the back as you pass,
But your final reward will be heartaches and tears
If you've cheated the guy in the glass.

—Dale Wimbrow, 1934

The message behind the image of the mirror is the foundation for training your mind to be disciplined and living life like you are dying. You must challenge yourself. This is a full-time commitment, 7 days a week, 365 days a year. You need to continuously motivate yourself, remain focused, and at times sacrifice many things to achieve self-mastery (see my book titled *Going from Undisciplined to Self-Mastery*).

It cannot be achieved with a part-time effort. That is why so many people fail to accomplish their goals. It must be part of your daily routine, just like putting your clothes on in the morning, or eating a meal.

Yes I am focused on Harris Kern 24x7 and guess who benefits—my family. The reality is no one at the end of the day is going to help me pay my bills, feed my kids, send them to college or accomplish my goals. Every day when I wake up I look in my imaginary mirror and go into battle with myself. I beat myself up mentally to adhere to my priorities and to conquer my goals at an accelerated rate. There's a sense of urgency every day of my life. Life is a one-time event and I make every minute count.

Focus most of your resources on developing yourself and being the best *you* can be. Don't spend countless hours worrying about spending time with your friends or acquaintances. Please don't misinterpret what I'm saying. I am not telling you to ignore your friends. You need to spend *some* time with them, but the reality is the friends you have now may not be around in five, ten years from now. Worry about yourself first. My daughter, who is eighteen, spends an exorbitant amount of time worrying about her friends and tends to forget about what really matters in life. She doesn't realize that most of her friends that she spends so much time with will probably not be around in the future.

Another important message from the guy in the mirror is that you should open the door to your mind every day and take a snapshot of the goals you want to accomplish. The thing to remember when going down this path is not to just merely achieve your goals on schedule—never just "meet" a goal's due date. The objective is to shatter that goal. Always try to outperform your previous best. Do whatever it takes. However, remember, the competition is only you.

Judge your progress by no one else's standards or accomplishments. That is what it takes to achieve self-mastery: a constant one-on-one dialogue (see the section on "Training the Mind"). Maintaining discipline is a constant battle, and your reflection is the enemy—your greatest challenge.

It is also important for you to consistently remind yourself that the body and mind must be one. You cannot separate the two. To separate the two will surely mean failure. Your body needs your mind, and your mind needs your body. You need to take care of both. Yes, that means exercising and eating right. You need the whole package behind you to be successful. Come on, get off your rear end and do something with your life! God gave you the tools. Why not use them to their utmost? Do not just sit there and exist. To subsist is boring. Go for it! What do you have to lose? Think once again about seeing a reflection of yourself in the mirror.

*Accomplishments are fulfilling, relaxation is a temporary feeling*

Life is all about accomplishments. There is no greater feeling in the world than achieving your greatest aspirations. Without accomplishments, you're just existing. With accomplishments you live and grow—life is worthwhile. Develop your mind as well as your body by training it to manage your life efficiently. Accomplishments (major and minor goals) are forever engraved and are a *huge* turn-on that last an eternity. I remember every one of my major and minor accomplishments, even the ones accomplished almost five decades ago.

We all need to relax, and I do as well. However, it's not what turns me on and it shouldn't turn you on either. Relaxation is a necessity to accomplish more to recharge those batteries so you can continue to be productive, but most people overdo it by relaxing way too much, and rarely accomplish anything, as time is just flushed down the toilet.

*Status quo is no different than death*

Doing the same routine day in and day out, year after year— how boring that must be. Get real, get on with it—time is so precious, if your life is stagnant, make something happen by introducing change. In business, when sales are down, you introduce change. If you're no longer as productive as you should be, introduce change into your routine.

*Content-free speech*

These are people that are good talkers, but have no substance behind their words. You know those individuals that promise the world but never deliver. This is prevalent in the corporate world, but also outside those office buildings. People love to talk and promise the world. Please don't go there—do as you say.

*Do I want to look like millions of other out of shape people?*

Exercising consistently is challenging—it's mostly mental toughness. You need to train the mind as well as the body equally. When I train someone I am constantly teaching them how to play mind games to help them train their mind. I ask them, "How badly do you want to change the way you look?" Or "Do you want to look like most out-of-shape people? Look at all of your co-workers, friends and family—do you want to look like them?"

I'm not saying this in a disrespectful way—I'm just playing mind games to train their mind to consistently motivate themselves. As highlighted throughout this book, there are many ways to train the mind to exercise consistently.

*Don't dwell on it*

When personal issues arise regardless of the severity, don't dwell on it. You're wasting precious time. Get over it quickly and get on with your life. If you can't walk away or let go of the issue and you feel that strongly about it, don't sit there whining and complaining—do something about it. When you've trained your mind to hold yourself accountable, your mind won't let you dwell on anything. It's pushing you to operate with a sense of urgency every day. It's on a mission to keep you focused on your priorities, goals and milestones.

*Never give up*

"It's always too early to quit."

**Norman Vincent Peale**

Whatever challenges you take on, regardless of the obstacles that lie before you, or the degree of difficulty, if you want it and you've planned appropriately, then be persistent—don't quit. There's no greater feeling than accomplishing a major goal.

*Treat every day equally*

In this era, everyone has been asked to do more with less as I mentioned in the beginning of the book. Very few people can actually take the entire weekend off and do whatever they want, or perhaps do nothing on Sunday but watch sporting events. Unfortunately, their projects, obligations and myriad activities inhibit them from truly enjoying time off.

The workload is immense and never-ending. If you remain structured and treat every day equally by following your priorities, to-do list, routine and focusing on your milestones first, every day you will be much more productive, therefore having more time to relax and do nothing—if that pleases you.

*Oh those endless excuses (i.e., this hurts, I feel sick, or I am feeling tired). If I wasn't disciplined I would rarely exercise*

When you're physically active and in your sixties like I am, occasional aches and pains become a way of life. I'm speaking from experience of going to the gym seven days a week. Exercise through these minor discomforts, otherwise they will become just another reason for abandoning exercise altogether. You know how I feel about that!

*It is what it is—keep moving forward*

The unexpected happens frequently and when you least expect it. These situations are oftentimes out of your control. What happened has already come to light, so don't dwell on the unexpected, and get on with it. You have your daily to-do list and routine to follow—just make it happen.

## MY FAVORITE GRIEVANCES

*Cell phones in the gym*

When it's time to exercise, make every moment count, especially if health and fitness are one of your priorities. Although I have a cell phone and use it profusely, I keep it in the car while working out—I am there for one reason only. It's very distracting to hear phones ringing. It's even worse having to listen to someone gabbing away while you're trying to focus and concentrate. Please keep them out of the gym as a courtesy to others; they really are annoying. Besides, what's more important? The next text message, call, etc., or focusing on your exercise routine?

*Personal trainers and the undisciplined*

Personal trainers are great for beginners. This is especially true when someone doesn't know the routine or the equipment. That's the positive; the negative is becoming dependent on a personal trainer. This is how personal trainers thrive. They know their clients don't have the discipline and motivation to make it happen on their own. They can just pay someone to push them.

Break the cycle and get disciplined. Follow the five steps highlighted in my book titled *Going from Undisciplined to Self-mastery* to develop your self-discipline skills, and train your mind to hold yourself accountable. It's equally important to train your mind as your body. Do not hire a trainer for more than six weeks. Once you understand the routine and are familiar with the equipment, then you should cut the cord and start motivating yourself.

*Don't use escalators or automated walkways when you're always complaining that you don't have time to exercise*

Executives who travel frequently complain that it's almost impossible to exercise when travelling. Hogwash! I have a hard time swallowing the fact that anyone can't find thirty minutes each day to exercise. There's always time to get some type of exercise in even if you have a busy schedule. The best time to consistently exercise is in the morning before going to work or taking that early morning flight. If you legitimately don't have the time, there are many alternative methods to get in some exercise throughout the day.

- Many of the buildings I visit have only two, three, four or five flights of stairs—so take those stairs—every little bit of activity counts. Don't be lazy.
- The same goes for departmental stores, subway stations or airports. Take the stairs whenever possible.
- Walk around your office building at lunch time if the weather permits.
- Do some sit-ups and push-ups in the morning before leaving your house.

Your body will thank you. As a frequent flyer, you definitely want to get as much exercise as possible before sitting on that long flight. I travel every other week and I still hand-carry my garment bag and computer bag while walking at a brisk pace, without the aid of automated walkways. Most people today are pulling their bags on wheels and walking on automated walkways. What's really pathetic is seeing grown men pulling their briefcases with wheels now. Give me a break...and you don't have time to exercise. Only utilize automated walkways when it's impossible to carry everything yourself.

*Feeling sorry for yourself*

Whether you're having a bad day at work, a fight with your significant other or you're a bit under the weather, feeling sorry for yourself or having other people pity you will only make matters worse. The more mentally tough you are, the faster you'll recover. Once your mind is trained, it will help you recover from a bad hair day much faster.

*Going to the doctor for every little ache and pain*

Every time this friend of mine caught a cold or had a new ache or pain, she went to the doctor. Is her behavior right? No—first of all, there are no cures for the common cold. Why waste your time for every little ache? I'm sure you can find more useful things to occupy your time. On the other hand, I went twenty years without going to a doctor. Now, is my behavior right? No, when you're over forty, you should go at least once a year for a physical. I should listen to my own advice—I'm over sixty and I still don't want to go on an annual basis.

*Children using backpacks with wheels when they don't need them*

What's this world coming to? No wonder there are so many children that are overweight, out of shape, lazy and don't feel the need to exercise. Wheeled backpacks were created for those years when the load of books may have been too much for a child who would be walking a good distance. Some young children were developing back problems because the weight of their books was too much for them, and this was a good solution. But in most cases they are not being used for these circumstances.

Use common sense here. You might ask yourself what difference it makes whether or not a child carries their books. Children need all the exercise they can get. Even worse are those parents and grandparents who carry their backpacks for them. It also sets a bad precedent for years to come. As these kids get older, they will continue to be lazy. Make them carry their books.

*Having an ego*

> "Don't let your ego get too close to your position, so
> that if your position gets shot down,
> your ego doesn't go with it."

### Colin Powell

When you live life like you are dying, the accomplishments keep piling up and your confidence level will soar. There's a high probability that you will start to get arrogant. You will feel like you're better than most—almost super-human. How do I know this? Yes, it happened to me. I'll make it simple—don't go there. Being disciplined and living life with a sense of urgency will get you to a place of success you could never imagine. You have an edge over so many people, but always be humble and learn to use your success in a positive manner—never let it get to your head.

# Acknowledgments

To my wife, Mayra, and our kids (Chade, Christian, CJ and Kevin) for bringing me so much joy and happiness.

To Leticia Gomez for being a genuine friend and business associate.

To Tony Potter for bringing this book idea to the forefront.

# About the Author

**Harris Kern** is one of the world's leading organization performance mentors (www.disciplinetheorganization.com) and personal mentors (www.disciplinementor.com). He is a frequent speaker at business, leadership and management conferences. His passion is to help people excel in their professional and personal life by helping them develop their self-discipline skills to combat top issues: severe procrastination, poor time management, ineffective goal management, lack of focus, no sense of urgency and being unmotivated. He also helps individuals improve their EQ skills (communication, relationship management and interpersonal) and leadership skills. He pioneered the *Discipline Mentoring Program* and *Professional/Personal Growth Program* (P²GP). Mr Kern is also the author of over forty books, some of the titles including:

- DISCIPLINE: Six Steps to Unleashing Your Hidden Potential
- DISCIPLINE: Training the Mind to Manage Your Life
- DISCIPLINE: Mentoring Children for Success
- DISCIPLINE: Take Control of Your Life
- Going From Undisciplined to Self-Mastery: Five Simple Steps to Get You There
- On Being a Workaholic: Using Balance and Discipline to Live a Better and More Efficient Life.

Mr Kern is recognized as the foremost authority on providing practical guidance for solving management issues and challenges. He has devoted over thirty years helping professionals build competitive organizations. His client list reads like a who's who of American and International Business. His client list includes Standard & Poor's, GE, The Weather Channel, NEWS Corporation and Hong Kong Air Cargo Terminal (HACTL) among hundreds of other Fortune 500 and Global 2000 companies.

Mr Kern is the founder and driving force behind the Enterprise Computing Institute www.harriskern.com and the bestselling series of Information Technology (IT) books published by Prentice Hall/Pearson. As founder of the Enterprise Computing Institute, he has brought together the industry's leading minds to publish "how to" textbooks on the critical issues the IT industry faces. The series includes titles such as:

- IT Services
- CIO Wisdom, CIO Wisdom II
- Managing IT as an investment, among others

Mr Kern's goal is to arm individuals and organizations with the tools to empower them to become more productive and successful.

## ADDITIONAL PERSONAL INFORMATION

Mr Kern lives every day with a **sense of urgency**! Life is short and he makes use of every minute, NOT hour or day! Mr Kern has been productive and successful for over forty years. He pushes himself extremely hard (by choice):

- Exercises every day of the year
- Has traveled to every continent and hundreds of cities all over the world (some several times)
- Established several successful businesses
- Purchased first home at the age of nineteen in the San Francisco Bay Area
- Raised a wonderful family
- Trained his mind and body to sleep four hours a night
- Financially set at the age of thirty-eight
- Graced the cover of *Hot Rod* magazine with his muscle car and speed boat at the age of twenty-one (July 1975 issue)
- Climbed the corporate ladder of a multi-billion dollar company without a formal college education at the age of thirty-one.
- Published dozens of books through his own imprint with the largest publishing company in the world.

Most people would consider his daily routine crazy and unhealthy, however, Mr Kern is sixty years old and he has mastered the ultimate level of discipline since his early twenties. Mr Kern believes that the body and mind should be pushed to the max every single day. The difference is, he has the experience to do so; however, Mr Kern would never push his clients in this manner unless of course this is their wish.

Mr Kern's greatest assets are his caring demeanor, incomparable energy and desire to help people manage their life efficiently. He wants to help as many people as possible fulfil their goals and aspirations.

Mr Kern can be reached at harris@harriskern.com or feel free to call him at 818.404.9248